MOVIE

IN

A

BOOK

THE
PRICELESS
CHINESE MAID
IN
AMERICA

TENI ABEGUNDE

CATAPHRASE MIAB
WWW.CATAPHRASE.COM

Printed in the United States of America.
V11/CP1245-110
000000009:13 Cataphrase MIAB
ISBN: 978-0-9916306-1-5 (Paperback Edition)

09-13-03-10-01-02-18

About the Author

You must be thinking you're about to read my biography after seeing "About the Author." The last time I attempted to write my biography, I ended up writing a book. What I meant by "About the Author" was, you know, the things about me you won't read on www.cataphrase.com.

My friends would describe me as cool—if I had any. I'm not sure what cool really means, but I'm sure it's not what you'll see if you hit me with a baseball bat. Perhaps it means you're more likely to see snow in July than to see me on a dance floor. Don't get me wrong, I like to party. I just don't dance unless I'm drunk.

I don't mean to state the obvious, but I'm assuming you already suspected that I'm a shy person. *Okay*, I'm not antisocial if that's what you're thinking. I have a Facebook account; I just don't remember my password.

I was born in Washington, D.C., a part of America where people walk when it's raining and jog when it's sunny. I don't know if I should call this behavior "the Capitol swag" or the ironic definition of cool. I have to ask a Washingtonian—I don't live there. I live next door in Maryland.

Occasionally, I'm a Redskin Raven. *Not the raven that flies*, in case you're wondering how a raven wrote a book. I'm not a bird. Redskin Raven is what you call a Redskins and Ravens fan.

The idea of Cataphrase started in 2013. It became official in 2014, when I wrote *Mercy McCurious* (the first Cataphrase book). As the founder of Cataphrase (movie in a book), a realist, and an author, I'm proud to say that, above all, I'm an American.

Author's signature page.

Cataphrase A

Cataphrase B

Cataphrase C

Cataphrase D

Cataphrase E

Cataphrase A

> "When you open a book, you open
> the mind of the author."
>
> —Teni A.

Scene 1

When you mention China to most Americans who haven't been there before, the first thing that might come to their minds is the ancient Asian architecture, like the red temples with curved roofs, the type they see on a menu when they order Chinese food. And of course, everyone knows that China is the land of chopsticks and the home of unlimited noodles.

To the rest of the world, China is just a magnificent, overpopulated country, one where everything is made. That's what most people think of China until they actually go there.

In truth, China boasts some of the best modern buildings in the world, a fast-growing economy, and top-of-the-line technologies.

However, just like some Americans can't afford a burger, noodles don't always come easily to all Chinese people.

[Scene 2]

Mei Chan, a nineteen-year-old damsel from Huizhou, had been standing in line at a local soup kitchen for thirty minutes. Twenty or so people stood in front of her. It wasn't her first time standing that long; she was used to it. Moreover, she couldn't afford to miss lunch that day. Beef brisket noodle soup was her favorite, and it was only served once a month.

But, missing her favorite food that afternoon wasn't her main concern; it was the dude standing behind her who was more interested in getting to know her than the free food he'd come to collect. The only way she could avoid the annoying voice of the pedophile behind her was to move to the second line, where they charged half-price. Otherwise, if she wanted a free lunch, she'd have to remain in front of him.

Her mind battled with the thought as she anxiously awaited her turn

There was a newspaper stand ahead, where a couple of people had gathered after they'd received their food. Out of curiosity, Mei also stopped by after she'd collected her food to see why everyone was attracted to the newspaper.

Someone behind Mei (in Chinese): "Nice paper, huh?"

She shrugged and turned her face to see who was speaking. The annoying dude who'd been standing behind her earlier was still following her. She hastened out of the kitchen with a copy of the newspaper covering her food.

[Scene 3]

The distance from the kitchen to Mei's house was about ten blocks. That was enough time to read the front page of the newspaper before she got home. But before she could turn the first page, a sign along the road caught her attention. It read: "A new cell phone manufacturing company in Beijing will be recruiting two hundred people in the next two weeks." Mei jotted down the company's number and planned to contact them when she got home.

[Scene 4]

The Chan family lived in a low-income neighborhood of Boluo County in Huizhou. Mei's father was a cab driver, and her mother worked nearby as a tailor. With four kids in a two-bedroom bungalow, sometimes it was hard for Mei's parents to pay the rent and still put food on the table.

Mei, the youngest child of the family, had always dreamed of traveling to the big cities and finding a good job. She spoke a little English and had a high school diploma. College was too expensive, though, so no one in the family bothered going there after high school.

[Scene 5]

Five yuan was all Mei had that afternoon when she arrived home. Hoping it would be enough to make at least a three-minute phone call, she went to the nearest pay phone on the next street.

[Scene 6]

The recruiter on the phone spoke in Chinese, but he added a little English. More than seven thousand people had already applied for the position. Mei's chances of getting the job were slim. However, after considering her level of English, the recruiter gave her a number to call. There was another branch in Huizhou that needed people who could speak English.

Mei wouldn't be able to make another call that afternoon, as she'd spent all her five yuan talking to the recruiter. She walked back home to join her family for the afternoon fishing.

[Scene 7]

[The next day]

Mei's house duties every morning were sweeping and washing dishes. A newspaper sat on the living room floor where the broom she was looking for stood. She recognized the paper as the one she'd brought from the soup kitchen the day before. Finally, she had a moment to flip the first page. The second page read: "KimCathy is offering a one-time opportunity to travel abroad." The requirement was simple: speak a little English, and in five months or less, you might be on a plane to America or Paris.

Nothing in life comes easy, Mei thought. But if the ad wasn't true, it won't be printed in *People's Daily*.

The last place on earth Mei ever dreamt of traveling to was the U.S.A. Where would a Chinese girl who couldn't afford breakfast get the money to buy a plane ticket, let alone live in a foreign country. She hadn't even set foot in Beijing before.

[Scene 8]

Mei thought about the ad, and the following day, she discussed it with her parents. According to her father, any opportunity that didn't cost a dime was worth trying.

[Scene 9]

Two days later, Mei responded to the ad, and the following week, she was selected for an interview in Shenzhen.

Though the ad didn't provide details as to what the traveling was about, an opportunity like that only comes once in a lifetime. Whatever it might be, Mei believed it would be better than the life she was living in Boluo.

[Scene 10]

Mei was on the first train to Shenzhen the day before her interview. With the little money her parents had borrowed to pay for her trip there, she planned to stay at a local motel and return the day after the interview.

Once she arrived at KimCathy's office in Shenzhen, Mei learned that it was a company that helped local Chinese people travel to foreign countries like the United States on the agreement that the person would work for them in the country without pay. That didn't sound too bad to Mei, as long as they fulfilled their promise to take care of her clothing, food, and accommodation.

[Scene 11]

After Mei completed the one-on-one interview, a representative took her picture and collected all other contact information before she returned home.

She wouldn't be hearing from KimCathy for another two months. Until then, all she could do was wait and hope that her dreams came true.

Mei had always been optimistic despite her poor background. With her natural Asian beauty, naturally highlighted hair, and incredible curves, she knew there was a place for her in the cities. She just didn't know how on earth she was going to get there.

[Scene 12]

To Mei's excitement, KimCathy followed through. She'd been accepted. When the time came, Mei spoke enough English to get through her America visa interview at the United States embassy in Beijing.

[Scene 13]

Less than four months after the whole process began, Mei was on her way to Shenzhen International Airport to board a plane heading for New York City. Her whole family was there to see her off.

[Scene 14]

The excitement in Mei's heart at the airport that evening was beyond description, yet the pain of separating from her family lingered on her face.

You didn't have to be a genius to know someone in the Chan family was traveling for the first time. Mei's luggage consisted of two jumbo laundry shopping bags.

[Scene 15]

When all other travelers were processing their baggage at the check-in counter, the Chans wandered around, trying to figure out where Mei would board her plane. It took the help of four good Samaritans to make sure Mei didn't miss her flight.

[Scene 16]

At 11:35 p.m., Mei hugged her family for the last time and proceeded to the final terminal checkpoint.

[Scene 17]

[Inside the airplane]

During the flight, Mei couldn't sleep. The view outside the window when the plane reached thirty thousand feet above the ocean was dark yet intriguing. Her left palm rested on the round airplane window as she stared outside, until a flight attendant distracted her with a dinner menu. She ordered every item of food and drink the crew had to offer.

[Twelve hours later]

When the pilot announced that the plane would be touching down in New York City in ten minutes, Mei was overwhelmed with joy, so much so that, when the time came to exit the plane, she nearly jumped over the passengers sitting next to her to get out of her row.

[Scene 18]

The flight from Shenzhen International Airport to JFK Airport in New York City had lasted approximately thirteen hours. Someone from the KimCathy company was waiting at the airport to pick Mei up.

Contact was made the old-fashioned way. The driver held up a sign that read "Mei Chan" and walked around the point where arriving passengers were coming out of the terminal.

Mei saw a man holding a sign with her name on it, and she approached him.

Mei: "Excuse me, are you here to pick me up?"

Driver: "Is this your name on my sign?"

Mei: "Yes, I just arrived from China."

Driver: "That's obvious. Can I see your international passport, please?"

Mei: "Sorry, I don't have it."

Driver: "Okay, that's not possible. If you don't have an international passport, there's no way you would have gotten past the immigration checkpoint. *Passport,* the little Chinese book that carries your name and your picture, can I see it?"

Mei reached in her bag to remove something.

Mei: "Oh, sorry, I have it. This one?"

Driver: "Yes, that one. I just need to verify your name."

The driver collected Mei's passport and verified her name.

Driver: "All right, Mei, welcome to America. My name is Randy Hill. I work for KimCathy. I'll be dropping you off at the KimCathy guesthouse in Manhattan. Someone is waiting there to meet you."

Mei: "Thank you."

Randy: "You're welcome."

[Scene 19]

Randy and Mei were in the car heading to Manhattan. Mei was sitting in the back seat.

Randy: "I was told to buy you food on the way if you are hungry. Are you hungry?"

Mei: "No. Yes. No."

Randy: "Which one is it—yes, no, or yes?"

Mei (with a smile): "Yes."

Randy: "All right. What would you like to eat?"

Mei: "Beef brisket soup."

Randy: "I don't know what that is, but we can stop at McDonald's if you don't mind. Do you like McDonald's?"

Mei: "Okay."

Randy: "'Okay.' I'll take that as a yes."

After they left the McDonald's drive-through, Mei sat quietly in the back seat with her bulky hand luggage, feeding her eyes with the wonderful view of New York City.

Randy had been picking up arrivals all morning for KimCathy, but something about Mei was different. He couldn't help but notice her outstanding beauty. Every little chance he had, he'd gazed in the rear-view mirror to get a glimpse of Mei's face and blonde hair.

Randy: "Hey, Mei, I was just wondering, are you a model?"

Mei: "No, I'm Mei."

Randy: "I know. What I'm asking is, are you here to work as a model? In other words, do you get paid when people take your picture and use it to advertise?"

Mei: "I'm sorry, I don't know. I came to America to work. I have a picture in my bag if you want to see it."

Randy: "Sure, I would love to."

Mei reached into her bag and brought out a photograph. She passed it to Randy.

Mei: "Here is the picture."

Randy gazed at the photo.

Randy: "Wow, how old were you when you took this picture?"

Mei: "I was seventeen. That's me in the middle, my mother on the left, and those are my two sisters."

Randy: "You are beautiful."

Mei: "Thanks."

[Scene 20]

[Forty minutes later]

Randy and Mei arrived in the parking lot of KimCathy's guesthouse in Manhattan.

Randy: "Here we are. Welcome to your new home. Let me assist you with your luggage. I hope Mrs. Ashley is still inside, or else I'll have to wait for her to return before I clock out."

[Scene 21]

[Inside KimCathy's guesthouse]

Randy: "Hi, Mrs. Ashley, *thank God* you are still here. I'm gonna clock out with the receptionist when Mei finishes removing her luggage from the trunk."

Ashley: "That's fine, thanks for your help. I'll need you again tomorrow afternoon to pick up more arrivals."

Randy: "All right, Mrs. Ashley, I'll see you tomorrow."

Ashley: "Thanks. Hey, Mei, how was your flight?"

Mei: "Good. I enjoyed myself."

Ashley: "Good, I'm glad to hear that. My name is Ashley. I'm one of the coordinators here at KimCathy. You can follow me upstairs. Let me show you where you'll be staying."

[Scene 22]

To Mei, being in America was like finding her vocation. Alone in a foreign country without someone telling her what to do, the teenage sense of freedom dawned on her.

That night, she was assigned a room on the fourth floor with another Chinese girl named Ai. Both of them had come to the United States for the same reason. Their room had a view of the ostentatious downtown streets of Manhattan, which were waiting to be explored.

[Scene 23]

Mei's first night in the guesthouse was filled with introductions. Hours passed like seconds.

When Mei remembered she hadn't called her family in China to inform them she'd arrived safely in America, it was already past midnight. She ran downstairs to use the phone in the lobby.

[Scene 24]

[Lobby]

The time in China then was around 12:23 p.m. There was a neighbor living next to the Chans' house in Boluo who had a house phone. Hopefully, someone was at home to pick it up. After several attempts with no one answering, Mei left a voicemail.

[Scene 25]

Mrs. Ashley returned the next morning to transport Mei and Ai to KimCathy's office in Lacrosse, where they would receive training for two weeks before their employment started.

[Scene 26]

At that office, when Mei arrived, several other Asian ladies were receiving training. It was in that moment that the reality of why she'd come to the United States started to sink in.

Mei needed to learn basic American communication, like how to provide customer service and how to communicate with customers.

KimCathy provided cleaning services for clients such as restaurants, office buildings, and family homes. They were also used by wealthy clients who needed maids or babysitters.

On Mei's first day at the training office, before she started training, she signed a bunch of papers. There, she learned her visa expired after two years. Her contract with KimCathy would also end when her visa expired, unless she was able to secure another year of stay through the American embassy.

[Scene 27]

After a few days of training, Mei had learned how to ride the train from the guesthouse where she stayed to the training office. As part of her compensation, the company gave her a cell phone.

[Scene 28]

One evening, after Ai and Mei finished training, they decided to stop at a Chinese restaurant before heading home. They were searching the menu for what they could afford when Mei's phone rang. Someone at the training center told them to return to the office immediately.

The holiday season was a busy time for KimCathy. Towards the end of the year, they receive more requests from most of their clients.

[Scene 29]

[Inside KimCathy's office in Lacrosse]

Fred Dunkin, who'd come on behalf of a wealthy client, waited at the office for the last two ladies to return. The moment Mei and Ai walked in the door, Fred had no doubt that Mei was the kind of maid his client would prefer. Mei spoke English better than the other Chinese ladies at the training center.

Fred signed Mei's contract at the manager's office, and in a matter of minutes, Mei was on her way to the house of one of the richest families in the world.

[Scene 30]

Smith Jones owned and controlled some of the largest oil refineries in North America and in the Middle East. His family was estimated to be worth around twenty-three billion U.S. dollars. Sharon Jones, Smith's wife, traveled a lot, but around the holiday season, she was usually at home in New York City, preparing for the holidays.

Amy, Jason, and Gary, the three children of the family, would also be at home for the holidays. That year, the Jones family would be hosting a royal family from the Middle East, another wealthy mogul. Mei would be staying with the family full time until the holiday season was over.

[Scene 31]

The beauty of the Jones mansion radiated from afar as the Cadillac SUV carrying Mei approached the gate.

[Scene 32]

[Inside the Jones mansion]

Mrs. Sharon wasn't at home to meet Mei, but there was another housekeeper who needed Mei to help out in the kitchen right away. The Jones family would be having a big dinner later that night.

[Scene 33]

Jason, the youngest of the family, walked in from football practice. He was heading to his room, but first, he wanted a glass of water. That was what brought him to the kitchen when he first saw Mei. His thirst disappeared at the sight of her alluring beauty.

Jason (to Mei): "Are you Amy's friend?"

Mei: "No."

Jason: "I haven't seen you before."

Housekeeper (interrupting): "She's not Amy's friend. Her name is Mei. She's the new housemaid."

Jason: "Nice to meet you, Mei. I'm Jason."

Mei: "Nice to meet you, too."

After the short introduction, Jason gave Mei a long look before going to his room.

Housekeeper (to Mei): "Mrs. Jones will be arriving soon.

She doesn't like to see any of the workers sitting on the couches in the house. And also, she's very sensitive to details, so make sure that, whatever you do, you do it right. Before I forget, do you smoke?"

Mei: "No."

Housekeeper: "Great. She doesn't like the smell of cigarettes either. When she comes back, she'll assign you a room. But for now, let's finish setting up the dining table. You'll see the rest of the family at dinner tonight."

[Scene 34]

The remaining members of the Jones family got home one after another.

Mrs. Jones could smell the truffles as she entered the house, but she didn't have time to stop in the kitchen. Her new dress would take all her attention that evening.

Amy had just bought a set of diamond jewelry she couldn't wait to try on. Gary was upstairs, busy with his little software project, while Mr. Jones was in his room, preparing for dinner. Jason couldn't wait to talk to Mei again.

[Scene 35]

Mei's bag was still at the guest living room where she'd left it before the housekeeper had asked her to help out in the kitchen. When she was done helping the cooks, she sat in the guest living room, across from the dinner table. Jason was the first person to arrive and notice her.

[Scene 36]

The rest of the Jones family arrived at the dinner table.

Jason: "Hey, Mei, come and join us."

Amy: "Who's Mei?"

Jason: "The new employee. I met her in the kitchen when I got home this evening."

Mei walked over to the dinner table.

Mrs. Jones: "I almost forget about her. Are you the maid from KimCathy?"

Mei: "Yes, ma'am."

Mrs. Jones: "Tell the housekeeper to give you the key to one of the vacant rooms in the guesthouse. I'll talk to you after dinner."

Jason: "Before she leaves, let her join us for dinner."

Mrs. Jones: "You can't be serious. You want a stranger to join us for dinner?"

Jason: "I don't see anything wrong with that. She got here a few hours before you guys arrived. She must be hungry, too."

Amy: "Isn't there food in the kitchen?"

Jason: "There is, but can she join us for dinner?"

Gary: "I'm cool with it. Hey, Mei, have a seat. Join us."

Mei attempted to sit at the dinner table, but Mrs. Jones responded with a frown.

Mrs. Jones: "Not there. That seat is meant for family members only. You can take what you want on the table and have a seat on the marble floor close to Amy."

Mei: "Thanks, ma'am."

Jason: "I'll sit wherever Mei does."

Amy: "And if she sits on the floor?"

Jason: "I'll sit on the floor."

Mr. Jones: "Darling, why can't the young lady sit at the table with us?"

Mrs. Jones: "You know I don't allow employees to sit on any of the couches or chairs in the house. They are very expensive."

Mr. Jones: "Can she? Just for the dinner, please? And Jason, since you invited a guest to join us, can you bless the dinner?"

Jason: "Sure. Lord, we thank you for this dinner. Thanks for providing it for us. Thanks for Dad, Mom, Amy, Gary, and thanks for Mei, the lady who is joining this family for the first time. She's not as rich as we are, but before you, oh Lord, we are all equal. We hold this truth to be self-evident, that all men are created equal, that they are endowed by their Creator with certain unalienable rights, that among these are life, liberty, and the pursuit of happiness. God forgive us all our sins and bless this dinner for Christ's sake. Amen."

Mr. Jones, Amy, and Gary: "Amen."

Amy showed Mei the right way to use the cutlery. The look on Mrs. Jones's face during dinner was ferocious. She constantly stared at Mei as if her presence at the dinner table would send the family into bankruptcy.

From the look on Jason's face when he made eye contact with her, Mei could sense that he liked her, but she couldn't be so sure.

Shortly after dinner started, Mei excused herself from the table and met with the housekeeper.

[Scene 37]

That night, around 11 p.m., Jason invited Mei to the garden behind the mansion. The half-moon and some shining little stars decorated the night sky as Jason took a walk with her in the garden.

Jason: "Mei, I apologize for my mom's behavior at the dining table earlier today. She didn't mean for you to sit on the floor. She was just upset about her new dress."

Mei: "No problem. It's okay. I'm used to it."

Jason: "You're used to what?"

Mei: "Sitting on the floor."

Jason: "All right, if you say so. What's your full name?"

Mei: "Mei Chan."

Jason: "Chinese?"

Mei: "Yes."

Jason: "How long have you been in America?"

Mei: "About a month now."

Jason: "Good. Welcome to America. How do you like it here?"

Mei: "Nice, I love America. It's beautiful."

Jason: "Thanks. I haven't been to China, but I heard there are some nice places over there, too. Mei, what brings you to America?"

Mei: "I came here to work."

Jason: "That's it?"

Mei: "Yes."

Jason: "How old are you?"

Mei: "Nineteen. You?"

Jason: "I'm twenty-three. Mei, there's something I want to tell you."

Mei: "What is it?"

Jason: "Can I hold your hand while we talk?"

Mei: "Okay."

Jason held Mei's hand as they strolled in the garden.

Jason: "You are beautiful."

Mei (with a smile): **"Thanks. You're handsome, too."**

Jason (also smiling): "Thanks. I try to stay in shape. Girls like it that way."

Mei: "You have a girlfriend?"

Jason: "I have a couple of female friends. I don't have a serious relationship with anyone. What about you? Were you dating a guy in China before you came here?"

Mei: "No. I'm still young. I've never dated anyone before."

Jason: "Amazing, I've never heard any girl say that."

Jason and Mei sat on the edge of a flowerbed.

Jason: "When I first saw you in the kitchen, I felt something in my heart. The feeling was as if I were standing in a pleasant place of harmony surrounded by calm waters, like a gentle river littered with roses and butterflies. Since the moment I met you, the feeling has been in my heart."

Mei (with a smile): "*That's* not true."

Jason: "How do you know?"

Mei: "Because the heart can't store feelings."

Jason: "Prove it."

Mei: "There was a woman in China who always told her son how much she loved him from the depths of her heart. The day the woman had a heart transplant, the boy was afraid that the next time his mom saw him, she wouldn't love him anymore.

"When the woman returned home from the hospital, the first question the boy asked her was: 'Mum, do you still love me from the depths of your heart?' She smiled and replied, 'Yes, son. I'll always love you.'

"There are only two ways that statement could be true. First is if the woman's heart was never replaced at the hospital, and second, if a human's heart isn't something that can store feelings."

Jason (with a smile): "That's funny. You know, I'd never thought about it. Okay, maybe not in my heart, but a feeling has been on my mind since I met you."

Mei: "Jason, I don't mean to stress your feelings, but where in the human body is the mind located?"

Jason: "That's a tricky question. Where do you think the mind is located?"

Mei: "What time is it?"

Jason: "It's 12:22 a.m. Why?"

Mei stood up and dusted off her skirt.

Mei: "I'm sorry, Jason, I have to go to bed now."

Jason: "Wait."

Jason stood up and moved closer to Mei.

Jason: "I'll be going out of town tomorrow for two weeks. I'll see you when I come back. Can I hug you?"

Mei: "Okay."

Jason hugged Mei for some seconds. When he released his arm, his lips came close to kissing Mei's forehead, but then Mei cleared her throat and left.

[Scene 37]

Mei had been in the Jones house for over two weeks now. Mrs. Jones was under the assumption that Mei was getting paid weekly; hence, no one had bothered to ask about her welfare. The majority of what she needed, like toothpaste and detergent, came from the housekeeper. Moreover, she had the weekends off to spend at KimCathy's guesthouse.

[Scene 38]

On Mei's second weekend off, she waited for someone from KimCathy to pick her up at the mansion. She needed to exit the mansion by 3 p.m. and hand over her room key to the housekeeper, but 2:45 p.m. passed, and no one had shown up.

[Scene 39]

At 2:54 p.m., Mei walked outside the mansion and stood at the gate.

An hour passed, and there was still no sign of KimCathy's driver. Mei called the guesthouse a few times, but no one answered the phone.

Mrs. Jones would be coming home soon. Mei knew the last person she would like to see standing at the entrance was a maid. She decided to stroll to the nearest bus stop. All she had left on her was five dollars. She had no plan to catch the bus.

[Scene 40]

The afternoon sky was getting cloudy. It seemed as if the rain would start at any time. Mei was looking at the bus stop three blocks away when she saw Jason's car heading in her direction.

Jason's Mercedes-Benz slowed down beside Mei. He rolled the window down.

Jason: "Where're you heading?"

Mei: "Home. My day off starts today."

Jason: "Do you live around here?"

Mei: "No. I live in downtown Manhattan. The person who was supposed to pick me up didn't show up."

Jason: "So, how're you gonna get home?"

Mei: "I don't know. Maybe I'll catch the bus."

The rain drizzled down.

Jason: "Hop in."

[Scene 41]

Mei got inside Jason's car.

Jason: "Are you cold?"

Mei: "I'm fine, thanks. Are you going home?"

Jason: "Yeah. I have to drop off my bags and take a shower. I was thinking you would prefer waiting in the house to standing outside in the rain."

Mei: "The housekeeper told me I can't stay in the house after 3 p.m. on my off day. I already gave her my room key."

Jason: "The housekeeper doesn't make the rules. I do. Don't worry. I'll talk to her."

Mei looked down as she sat in the front passenger seat.

Jason: "What's wrong?"

Mei: "What about your mum?"

Jason: "What about her?"

Mei: "Will you talk to her, too?"

Jason: "Is she at home?"

Mei: "She will be back soon."

Jason: "Don't worry. I'll talk to her. Is that all?"

Mei nodded.

Jason: "Have you eaten?"

Mei shook her head.

Jason spun the Mercedes-Benz around, making a U-turn.

Jason: "I've got something for you."

Mei smiled at the car's swift movement.

Mei: "Where're we going?"

Jason: "To the finest Chinese restaurant in New York City."

Mei: "No, I can't afford it. I only have five dollars on me."

Jason: "I can. I have a lot of money."

Cataphrase B

"I hate poverty more than death."

—Teni A.

[Scene 42]

[La Bergrill Asian seafood restaurant]

At the table, Jason ordered some expensive seafood and wine.

Jason: "How's the food?"

Mei: "Nice. I haven't dined at a nice restaurant like this before."

Jason: "There's always a first time for everything."

Mei: "Jason, why would a guy like you bring a maid to a beautiful restaurant like this?"

Jason: "You're not a maid."

Mei: "So, what am I?"

Jason: "You are the most beautiful Asian woman I've ever met. I brought you here because you're hungry."

Mei: "Thanks. But that's still not why you brought me to the best Chinese restaurant in New York and bought me the most expensive seafood in the world. There were other less expensive Chinese restaurants along the way, and I'm sure there are a lot of beautiful Asian women out there who look better than me. Why here? Why me?"

Jason looked Mei straight in the eyes.

Jason: "I love you."

Mei: "Prove it."

Jason got up, moved closer, and gave Mei a sudden kiss. His lips clung to hers for a good three seconds before he let go. Mei's eyes were closed for every second of the kiss. Her heart was beating rapidly.

It was Mei's first kiss. For a moment after the kiss, she didn't know if she should use the ladies' room or take another bite from the bluefin tuna in front of her. Jason was the first to speak.

Jason: "I don't know where the mind is located in the human body, but I know you've been on my mind since the last time we spoke in the garden. I hope I didn't scare you."

Mei: "I wasn't expecting it. No man has ever kissed me. Was that your first kiss?"

Jason: "No."

Mei nodded.

Jason: "Where do you plan to go when we finish here?"

Mei: "I'd love to go home if I can find someone to drop me off."

Jason: "Do you have any plans for the weekend?"

Mei: "No."

Jason: "Do you really have to go home?"

Mei: "No. Yes."

Mei and Jason laughed simultaneously.

Mei: "I'm not sure. I mean, where else will I go?"

Jason: "There's something I want to show you."

Mei: "What is it?"

Jason: "You'll find out when we get back in the car."

[Scene 43]

[Inside Jason's car]

Jason had a diamond necklace that his mother had given him on his twenty-first birthday. In his heart that evening, he believed Mei deserved the necklace more than him, as he had countless pieces of expensive jewelry at home.

Mei was speechless when he gave her the five-karat diamond necklace.

Neither of them had plans for the evening, so Jason decided to take Mei to an abandoned mansion on the other side of town.

The house was located in an isolated area of East Letch Park. Jason couldn't think of any place in town to take Mei that was more romantic than the mansion.

The evening was cool and breezy. The rain had just finished nourishing the earth. The mansion would be wet and adventurous.

Legend told horrific tales about the mansion, some of which included curses of death on whoever took something from inside the house.

Jason had read about it in a book and had visited once with a group of friends. Most of what he'd read about the house sounded like nothing more than mere fiction.

The joy of admiration filled Mei's heart, so much so that she didn't remember to ask Jason where he was taking her until they got there.

[Scene 44]

After twenty-five minutes of driving, Jason parked on the roadside and reached for his jacket in the back seat.

Mei: "Where are we?"

Jason: "There's a house around here I want to show you."

Mei: "Who lives there?"

Jason: "Nobody. Wear my jacket. I'll hold your hand as we walk."

[Scene 45]

Jason and Mei stepped out of the car.

Mei: "Who lives in the house?"

Jason: "Nobody. It's an abandoned house. I've read interesting stories about it."

Mei: "Are we going to be back before it gets dark?"

Jason: "Yeah, I promise."

[Scene 46]

Jason held Mei's hand as they walked frantically through the woods. Mei didn't know why the house was special to Jason. Before she could ask another question about it, an old, creepy abandoned house came into sight. The building was partially covered in shrubs.

[Scene 47]

Jason scrambled to remove his phone from his back pocket. The moon and Jason's little flashlight was their only source of light. Gradually, they closed the distance.

[Scene 48]

At the entrance of the house lay a gray stone with the

inscription: "To believe in life is to believe in death; for in the land of the dead, the soul lives. Tiamat laenatan lives here. Albany Museum of Art." The remaining inscriptions were written in Arabic.

The abandoned house had once belonged to Akar Amos, an Egyptian sorcerer who traveled around the world collecting possessed artifacts. One stone in particular, known as Tiamat, led him to the United States in the early 1940s. He'd heard of the curse and disease inflicted by the stone, and he came to offer help. As an experienced sorcerer, he knew the history of the stone and how to cure the afflictions it caused.

The Tiamat Stone was first brought to the United States by an American oceanographer who died from an unknown disease days after he found it in the ocean and brought it home to his family. Shortly after his death, everyone in the family who tried to remove the stone from the house died of the same disease.

By the time Akar finally revealed the cure for the curses and diseases brought by the stone, more than seventeen people had died from its terrible afflictions. He was later persuaded to help remove the stone and relocate it to an isolated part of Letch Park.

A year later, Akar died. He was buried in the house he built for himself and the stone in Letch Park.

Jason pointed the little flashlight on his phone to the text on the stone and read the English inscription.

Mei held Jason by the arm as he took the first step inside the house.

The only thing blocking the entrance were spider webs, which Jason removed with a wave of his hand. Everything inside the house appeared undisturbed. There were more Arabic words on the walls that Jason couldn't read. The decor inside the house resembled those used by ancient Egyptians.

[Scene 49]

[Inside one of the rooms]

Jason: "Look at the little pyramid over there on the table."

Jason and Mei moved closer to the table. Jason's flashlight illuminated the little carved golden pyramid containing more abstruse inscriptions like the ones on the walls.

Jason: "It's beautiful."

Mei rubbed the pyramid slowly with her finger.

Mei: "Nice."

Jason: "You like it?"

Mei nodded while comparing the pyramid with the gold chain that held the diamond pendant on her neck.

Jason: "There's something else here more beautiful than a golden pyramid and a diamond necklace."

Mei: "What is it?"

Jason: "You. Mei, do you love me?"

Mei (with a shy and gentle smile): "Yes."

Jason: "How do you know?"

Mei: "I can feel it in my heart."

Jason cleared the table with a swipe of his hand, lifted Mei up, and sat her on its surface. Their eyes locked for a moment before Jason went for a long kiss.

After a minute, Mei stopped the kiss. Something that hadn't been in the center of the room when they'd entered now shone brightly.

Mei: "Wait. What is that?"

Jason: "What?"

Mei pointed to the center of the room.

Mei: "Behind you."

Jason turned to look at what he thought was a person standing in the center of the room. Instead, what he saw was a shining, bulky green diamond that looked like a stone hanging in a birdcage. A bold English and Arabic sign on the cage read: "Do not touch."

Jason was excited. He believed the stone was an emerald. If he could examine it more closely, he thought, he might be able to tell if the stone was an ordinary stone or a gem. He couldn't resist the temptation of touching it.

The iridescent nature of the stone grew brighter as the light from Jason's phone struck it. One pull from a dangling string hanging below the cage was all it took to set the stone loose. Jason reached out and caught the stone before it hit the ground.

Just as the stone touched his palm, a tingling and burning sensation went through his body. The feeling stopped as soon as he let go of it.

Mei: "What happened?"

Jason: "I don't know. I felt a shock."

Mei: "Jason, you're bleeding."

Jason: "Where?"

Mei: "Your left nostril."

Jason wiped the blood coming from his nose with his shirt, and the bleeding stopped.

Mei: "I'm scared. We have to leave now. Are you okay?"

Jason: "I'm fine. Let's get out of here."

[Scene 49]

As they made their way back to the car, Jason began experiencing vertigo. Mei managed to help him out of the woods and called an ambulance on her cell phone.

[Scene 50]

Mei laid Jason at the roadside, beside the Mercedes-Benz.

Sheriff Cory, a law enforcement veteran with twenty-five years of experience working in Orange County, was the first to arrive at the scene. The moment he saw Jason's eyes, he knew right away what had happened.

The first month Cory was a sheriff, he'd responded to a similar situation. The two female tourists who'd last touched the stone had died at the hospital in less than a month. The greenish color he'd seen in the eyes of those two tourists twenty-five years ago was now in Jason's eyes, too. He turned to Mei.

Sheriff Cory: "Did anyone else touch the stone?"

Mei: "No, just him."

Sheriff Cory called for an ambulance on his radio.

More police vehicles arrived at the scene the same time as the ambulance.

Jason was transported to the nearest state hospital. Mei gave a statement to the police and left the hospital before the Jones family arrived.

[Scene 51]

The first doctor who examined Jason had never seen anything like his situation before. Every diagnostic test he ran came back negative.

Another physician, who specialized in biochemical attacks, suggested they transfer Jason to a federal military hospital in Virginia.

[Scene 52]

The doctors in Virginia came to the same conclusion. They'd never come across such an ailment in any patient before.

Dr. Charles, who worked for the Jones family, was forced to go back to the police report and reconsider the origin of the sickness.

The lack of belief in mythology caused all the doctors who examined Jason to dismiss the stone from being a possible cause. But Dr. Charles thought otherwise. With the reputation of the Jones family, it didn't take long to convince the state police to look into the case.

[Scene 53]

A group of police officers, scientists, and archeologists were deployed the following morning to investigate the house where Jason had touched the stone. The inscriptions on the stone at the entrance of the abandoned house pointed them to the Museum of Art in Albany, New York.

[Scene 54]

Dr. Charles and a police superintendent arrived at the Museum of Art in Albany the next morning. They met with Professor Anthony, who knew the history of the Tiamat Stone.

Professor Anthony was in his mid-seventies. He had gray hair, wore an old-fashioned monocle, and had a witty demeanor.

[Inside Professor Anthony's office]

Dr. Charles and Superintendent Carl were seated, waiting for Professor Anthony. The professor entered the room.

Professor Anthony: "Sorry for the wait. I'm Professor Anthony. What can I do for you gentlemen?"

Superintendent Carl: "I'm Superintendent Carl from the Orange County Police. This is Dr. Charles.

"An incident happened yesterday inside an abandoned house in Letch Park. Do you recognize the house in this picture?"

The superintendent passed a picture across the table to Professor Anthony.

Professor Anthony: "Holy Big Bang, not again. Please tell me nobody touched that creepy stone."

Superintendent Carl: "Someone did. He's at the hospital right now. The doctors couldn't diagnose him as having any known sickness. Professor, what do you know about this stone?"

Professor Anthony: "Well, gents, you've come to the right place. That stone is known as the Tiamat Stone, and it first surfaced in the United States about sixty-five years ago. It was found on the bed of the ocean by a deep-sea explorer in the early forties. Ever since the stone arrived in New York City, every human who has touched it has died in a matter of weeks.

"The creepy green devil was relocated to an isolated part of Letch Park some sixty-three years ago by an Egyptian sorcerer named Akar Amos. The last time I heard of the stone was twenty-five years ago, when two tourists from Spain stumbled into the house where it was kept in Letch Park."

Dr. Charles: "What happened to those tourists?"

Professor Anthony: "They kicked the bucket three weeks later in Spain. The story about the stone is more like superstition; thus, it has long been dismissed by the scientific community as a myth. But the good news is, Akar wrote a book about the Tiamat Stone before he died. The preternatural book contained details of how to cure the curses and diseases brought by the Tiamat. We have the book here on private display. The first week I got here, I attempted to read it. I dropped it faster than I picked it up."

Dr. Charles: "Why?"

Professor Anthony stood up.

Professor Anthony: "If you gentlemen will follow me, I can show you the book. Hopefully, one of you can make sense of it."

Dr. Charles and Superintendent Carl stood up.

Superintendent Carl (to Professor Anthony): "Please. After you."

[Scene 55]

Professor Anthony led the superintendent and Dr. Charles to the private historical relic display room. When they got there, Professor Anthony opened the display case and brought out the book. He handed it to Dr. Charles.

Professor Anthony: "There it is."

Dr. Charles opened the first page of the book.

Dr. Charles: "It's written in Arabic?"

Professor Anthony: "Just like the Quran. But this one is different. The book contains 777 pages, 177,777 words in total. It cost me two thousand precious U.S. dollars to convince a man who understands Arabic to translate the complete content of the book into the English language. At the end, what the author wrote is more complicated than what a human can translate. Most of the writing is based on human astrological attributes and magical chants. The most important of all is the cure for the curses and diseases brought by the Tiamat Stone. I knew a day like this would come, so I asked my translator to write the English version of the cure in a separate book."

Carl: "Where is the English version?"

Professor Anthony: "It comes with a price. The original Arabic version belongs to the museum. The translated version of the cure belongs to me. It will cost you five hundred bucks to own a copy. I have a copyright certificate for the English version if want to see it."

Dr. Charles: "Why didn't you discuss the cure with the science community?"

Professor Anthony: "After you pay me five hundred bucks, doctor, you will find out why. Gentlemen, I'll be in my office when you're ready."

[Scene 56]

The following morning, Mr. Jones and Dr. Charles returned to the museum.

[Inside Professor Anthony's office]

Professor Anthony: "Welcome, Mr. Jones. I remember Dr. Charles from yesterday. I didn't know he works for you."

Mr. Jones: "Where's the cure?"

Professor Anthony: "You mean the book."

Mr. Jones: "Yeah. That envelope on your desk contains a thousand dollars in cash. Professor, where is the book?"

Professor Anthony put his glasses on and looked inside the envelope.

Professor Anthony: "All right, gentlemen, give me a second. I'll be back."

After a few minutes, Professor Anthony handed the English version—a ten-page book containing Akar's cure-to Dr. Charles.

Professor Anthony: "Doctor, here's what you asked for. I hope you and your colleagues can figure out the meaning. I don't know how true that book is, but one thing is true—nineteen people died in less than a month after touching the Tiamat Stone. Good luck to your victim."

Mr. Jones: "He's my son."

Professor Anthony: "I'm sorry to hear that, Mr. Jones. I wish there was something I could do to help. Good luck to your son, sir."

Dr. Charles read aloud from the third page of the book.

Dr. Charles: "The ocean is the home of Tiamat. When it is removed from the ocean, air awakens its fury.

"Whosoever touches the Tiamat Stone before reciting the proper chant awakens the spirit of death. The victim will carry the green cursed disease for twenty-seven days before his death.

"A bite from an inland taipan, the chosen snake from the tribe of Abzu, Babylonian king of the abyss of saltwater, the husband of Tiamat, can be used to suppress the disease of Tiamat in a victim for seven days. Only an inland taipan and a virgin can cure the curse and disease of Tiamat.

"To begin the cure, the virgin, male or female, in the nude, must say the beautiful princess chant at the shore of a salty ocean.

I send the power
of the wind to you,

Mzui, beautiful
blue princess of the salty
ocean.
I summon you from
your dwelling place.
In the name of Raphael,
Rohi, and Rehoba, arise.
Bring to me the beauty
of Nymph and the healing
of Nodens. Take me to
the land beneath the
ocean. Show me the
four dreams of Amzirhote.
Samna El Abastani.

"This chant will ignite the four dreams of Amzirhote. The blue evidence will be seen in the eyes of the dreamer when he or she awakes.

"After the dream, the virgin must touch the Tiamat Stone. The virgin will also, as a result, be infected by the stone.

"An inland taipan must be chosen to bite the virgin twice. The same snake that bit the virgin must also bite the victim twice. When the venom enters their body, it will suppress the sickness for seven days. During these seven days of strength, the victim must copulate with the virgin for both of them to be cured, and they must drink from the ocean for the Tiamat curse to be completely removed."

Dr. Charles: "This is absurd."

Professor Anthony: "Absurd is a nice word compared to what I call it: a crime against humanity, absolutely preposterous."

Mr. Jones: "Who wrote this thing?"

Professor Anthony: "An Egyptian sorcerer named Akar Amos. He wrote the original Arabic version around sixty-three years ago."

Mr. Jones: "Professor, do you believe in this cure?"

Professor Anthony: "If I say yes, you should tell my supervisor to fire me on the spot. I'm a science professor, Mr. Jones. I don't believe in mythology.

"Inland taipans are the most venomous snakes on earth. One drop of venom from a taipan has enough toxin to kill one hundred grown men. Now, imagine the kind of damage that two bites will inflict on a human body."

Mr. Jones: "*All right*, let's talk about other options. What other cure exists for this disease other than this suicide mission written by a sorcerer?"

Professor Anthony: "That's where the problem lies, Mr. Jones. There *is* no other option or cure that exists for the Tiamat disease. The only cure ever recorded is what I just gave you."

Mr. Jones (angrily): "You mean this madness you sold me is the only hope my son has of surviving?"

Dr. Charles (interrupting): "Professor, has this cure ever been tested on any of the previous victims?"

Professor Anthony: "You mean has any virgin ever been stupid enough to volunteer themselves to be bitten twice by the world's deadliest snake? Is that the question you're asking me, Dr. Charles?"

[Short silence]

Mr. Jones stood up and reached for a handshake.

Mr. Jones: "It's been nice talking to you. You can keep the book; we won't need it anytime soon."

Professor Anthony: "It's been a pleasure meeting you, Mr. Jones. However, I would suggest that your doctor keep a copy of Akar's cure in case you change your mind. I don't believe in the cure, but I believe in the effect of touching the Tiamat Stone. Mr. Jones, if your son actually touched the stone, he has less than a month to live. Nineteen dead bodies are my witnesses."

Mr. Jones looked at Professor Anthony for some seconds before he and Dr. Charles left the office.

CATAPHRASE C

"Work hard and walk hard. Break your own little
fancy rules if you have to. Nature only favors
the strongest, not the cutest."

—Teni A.

[Scene 57]

[Reno State Hospital]

Three days had passed since Jason had fallen sick.

Mrs. Jones, Amy, Gary, and the New York City mayor were beside Jason's sickbed when Mr. Jones and Dr. Charles returned to the hospital.

Dr. Charles and Mr. Jones spoke to Dr. Morris, another private doctor, in Jason's room.

Charles: "How is he feeling?"

Dr. Morris: "He's not getting any better. His blood pressure rises abnormally every time he takes his medication."

Mr. Jones: "Where is the girl who was there when the incident happened? The maid. Where is she? I want her to explain to me how the whole thing happened."

Mrs. Jones: "I fired her yesterday. I don't want to ever see that girl again."

Mayor: "She was detained and released last night. I personally went to the abandoned house in Letch Park before midnight with some biochemical experts. One of the experts suggested that we test the stone with a rabbit. What happened to the rabbit was exactly what Mei claimed happened to Jason when he touched the stone. The rabbit's condition this morning was similar to Jason's. I've never seen anything like it before. I ordered the biochemical experts to secure the stone right away."

Mr. Jones: "So, this thing is real, huh?"

Mayor: "With what I saw happen to the rabbit yesterday, yes, it is."

Mr. Jones: "I have all the money in the world, but I can't help my son."

Dr. Morris: "Everything will be fine, Mr. Jones."

Mr. Jones: "Yeah, that's what everybody tells a rich man until it's too late. Charles, where's that thing?"

Dr. Charles: "What thing, sir?"

Mr. Jones: "The book, the godforsaken cure. The one the crazy professor sold us at the museum. Where is it?"

Charles: "It's in my briefcase."

Mrs. Jones: "Oh, thank God. You found a cure."

Mr. Jones: "Yeah, we did. Charles, show her the damn cure."

Mrs. Jones took the book containing Akar's cure from Dr. Charles and read it.

Mrs. Jones: "You've got to be kidding me."

Mr. Jones: "I wish I was."

Amy and Gary also took the small book and read the cure.

Amy and Gary: "This can't be real!"

They passed it to the mayor and Dr. Morris.

Mayor (after reading the cure): "Where did you say you got this book from?"

Dr. Charles: "We bought it from a science professor at the Museum of Art in Albany."

Mayor: "I don't know what kind of professor sold this book to you, but the fellow needs to be arrested. How could a science professor call this blunder a cure?"

Dr. Morris: "I agree with the mayor. Whoever wrote this book must be out of his mind."

Dr. Charles: "The professor didn't write it. The original book was written by an Egyptian sorcerer sixty-three years ago. The professor only translated the pages in the book that contained the cure."

Mr. Jones: "Mayor, I need to talk to you at your office when you're free."

[Scene 58]

[Inside KimCathy's guesthouse]

Mei was distressed. She couldn't stop crying. Mrs. Jones had called KimCathy and canceled her contract.

The Orange County Police had called KimCathy's guesthouse every day since the incident had occurred. KimCathy didn't want to get involved with the police, so they planned on sending Mei back to China. The good life Mei had dreamed of had begun to shatter less than two months after she'd arrived in America.

[Scene 59]

Mei lay on her bed alone in the room. She stayed up all night, till early morning. The shame of returning home penniless weighed on her mind. At the same time, she couldn't stop thinking about Jason. He was her first love, the man who'd given Mei her first kiss. The only valuable property she had was the necklace Jason had given her.

As Mei lay in bed, she stared at the clock with tears rolling down her cheeks, knowing she was just hours away from facing the consequences of the troubles Jason had gotten her into. Mrs. Ashley was coming in the morning to arrange Mei's flight back to China. It was either now or never. It would be better to be homeless in New York City than to be broke in Boluo.

Mei stepped out of bed and stuffed a couple of articles of clothing into a handbag. She looked around the room one more time, turned off the light, and exited the room.

She thought about leaving a note, but that would be unnecessary. KimCathy wasn't necessarily her guardian, and Mei had learned enough to know that a nineteen-year-old in America is considered grown enough to make his or her own decisions. If anyone from KimCathy wanted to talk to her, they had her number.

[Scene 59]

The five dollars in her purse that she'd gotten before Jason had taken her out for an expensive lunch was still there. She sat at a bus stop till early morning and rode the first bus out of Manhattan.

[Scene 60]

[At the New York City mayor's office]

The mayor entered the office where Mr. Jones was waiting.

Mayor (to Mr. Jones): "Sorry for keeping you waiting. I just got back from the governor's office. He sends his regards to your family. Mr. Jones, I wish there was something I could do to help."

Mr. Jones: "I want to make a public announcement."

Mayor: "Okay. I can help you with that. Do you want me to call the press? What is it about?"

Mr. Jones: "I'll give ten million dollars to any woman who will volunteer for the Akar cure. Yesterday, I paid some medical researchers to open a research program on the cure. They need a virgin who will volunteer."

Mayor: "Mr. Jones, you do understand that this so-called cure is not in any way scientific. The risk involved is more than—"

Mr. Jones (interrupting): "Twenty-five million dollars. For any woman who is willing to take the risk."

Mayor: "Mr. Jones, we are speaking of a human life—"

Mr. Jones (interrupting again): "Fifty million dollars."

Mayor: "All right, if that's what you want. I'm going to prepare the press and some doctors. Everything will be set by 4 p.m. today."

Mr. Jones: "Why call some doctors?"

Mayor: "They are the ones who will explain the risk involved to the public. Mr. Jones, with all due respect, I'm the mayor of the city of New York. I can't just allow you and your scientists to offer fifty million dollars to a female virgin without first explaining to her the complete truth about the risk she's going to be taking."

Mr. Jones: "That's fine. I'll call my medical researchers to meet me here before 4 p.m."

[Scene 61]

Mei had been wandering the streets of Harlem for over three hours. She'd soon find out that life on the street wasn't meant for her. Around 12 p.m., on the day she left KimCathy's guesthouse without notice, she scouted every little restaurant on the block of Ann Avenue in Harlem, looking for a cafeteria where her last three dollars would be enough to buy lunch.

[Scene 62]

The necklace around her neck was just too conspicuous. It was the first thing the clerk at Sam's carry-out noticed before he noticed that Mei still owed him seventy-five cents more for the sandwich she'd ordered.

Mei patted her pocket and searched her bag as if she didn't know all she had left was three dollars. She managed to persuade a guy standing next to her to pay for her lunch.

Clerk: "Nice jewelry."

Mei: "Thanks."

Clerk: "Hey, if you want to sell it, I know this guy down the street. His name is Kelly. He pays good money for gold and diamonds. Ask anyone around here; they'll show you where his shop is located. I used to work for him."

Mei: "Thanks, I'm not selling it."

Clerk: "I'm just saying."

Mei picked up her food and sat at a table inside the cafeteria. The thought of selling the necklace hadn't crossed her mind until the nosey clerk had brought it up. Selling it was a good idea to make some money, considering her situation, but Mei wasn't going to go that route anytime soon.

She was enjoying what seemed to be her last easy lunch when a familiar face appeared on the TV across the room from her table. Mr. Jones and his medical researchers were on. The mayor and two medical doctors stood next to them. The broadcast headline alone was enough to make any virgin female commit adultery. It read: "Medical researchers in New York are offering a fifty-million-dollar reward for a female volunteer. Volunteers must be chaste and eighteen or over to participate."

Mei wasn't sure what the broadcast was about. Mr. Jones

was a rich and famous person, so Mei thought it was just one of his business ventures.

However, another thought came to her mind. Could the broadcast be about Jason's situation?

The thought of Jason suddenly sprang up again in her mind, so strongly that she decided she needed to see him that evening. Mei didn't have a dime to her name, but somehow, she was going to find a way to get to the state hospital where Jason had been admitted.

The window where Mei sat had a good view of the street. Her next move was to come up with the money to ride a bus to Reno Hospital.

Her desperation brought an unusual thought: the Asian couple she saw outside the window might help if she told them her situation.

[Scene 63]

Mei tossed her paper plate in the trash and caught up with The couple before they entered their vehicle. After a short conversation, the couple gave Mei a ride to Reno Hospital.

[Scene 64]

[Outside Reno State Hospital]

A feeling of fear gripped Mei's heart outside the hospital entrance. If she ran into Mrs. Jones, only God knew what would happen. She summoned courage and made a bold move into the hospital.

Mr. Jones had paid an untold amount of money to the hospital's management to hand out copies of Akar's cure to all visitors. The hospital receptionists had done a good job of passing out the message.

[Scene 65]

Mei told the staff at the front desk she was Jason's girlfriend. One of the hospital receptionists handed Mei a copy of Akar's cure before directing her to Jason's private room.

The headline on the booklet was unmistakable. It was the same headline she'd seen on the news at Sam's carry-out. She read through the pages as she walked to Jason's room.

[Scene 66]

Jason was alone. The room was slightly dark. The television was on, and the bathroom door had been left open. Mei walked inside the room step by step until she came close to Jason.

Jason couldn't talk, but he could see Mei. She placed her left hand on his face while she held his hand with her other hand.

Mei (whispering in Jason's ear with tears in her eyes): "I love you."

As much as Mei wanted to stay, she had to leave. Mrs. Jones

could arrive at any time.

She was on her way out when her worst nightmare came true. Mrs. Jones, carrying a lunch bag, entered the room with Amy. Amy turned on the light, and Mei was caught standing right there in the middle of the room.

Mrs. Jones: "What are you doing here?"

Before Mei could reply, Amy responded.

Amy: "Is that Jason's necklace on her neck?"

Amy and Mrs. Jones moved closer to Mei.

Amy: "Oh my God, that's Jason's diamond necklace."

Mrs. Jones: "Call security."

Mei: "I didn't steal it. Jason gave it to me."

Amy: "He did what? He can't even move his fingers. I thought you were a good person when I first met you. You should be ashamed of yourself."

Jason heard the conversation. The most he could do was slowly move his face. Mei knew she was in serious trouble. The only person who could prove her innocence lay behind her, completely paralyzed.

The hospital security guards didn't have to dial 911. Two county policemen patrolled the hospital premises on a daily basis seven days a week. Mrs. Jones was the first to talk to the police when they arrived at the door.

Mrs. Jones: "That's the girl right there, the Asian one. She used to work in my house before I fired her. My daughter and I entered the room and saw her trying to leave with my son's diamond necklace."

First Police Officer: "Where is your son?"

Mrs. Jones: "That's him on the bed. He's been here for five days now. He's paralyzed."

Second Police Officer (to Mei): "Ma'am, what's your name?"

Mei: "Mei Chan."

Second Police Officer: "What are you doing here?"

Mei: "I came to visit Jason."

Mrs. Jones (interrupting): "She's a liar. She used to work in my house. I fired her. She's not supposed to be here."

Security Guard: "Hey, I remember you. You told the receptionist that you are Jason's girlfriend."

Amy: "Oh my God, she's such a freaking liar. She's not my brother's girlfriend. Why in the world would Jason date a maid?"

Second Police Officer: "Are you Jason's girlfriend?"

[Silence]

First Police Officer: "Mei, that necklace you're wearing, is it yours?"

Mrs. Jones (interrupting): "I bought it for Jason two years ago on his birthday. It's a five-karat pure diamond engraved in twenty-four-karat gold. It cost me eighteen thousand dollars."

First Police Officer: "Ma'am, let her answer the question."

Mei remained silent. She was crying while looking at Jason.

First Police Officer: "All right, Mei, turn around. You're under arrest."

The police took the necklace from Mei and handed it to Mrs. Jones. Mei's eyes were filled with tears.

[Scene 67]

[Outside the hospital]

The cops had no intention of locking Mei up. Officer Taylor (the first police officer) wasn't really sure if his probable cause was solid enough to book Mei. Officer

Patrick (the second police officer) believed there was more to the story than what they'd heard inside the hospital. Mei didn't have any form of identification with her and appeared innocent. She just didn't look like the type that would be desperate enough to rob a patient inside a hospital.

Officer Taylor gave Mei some advice and let her go outside the hospital.

[Scene 68]

Mei walked to the nearest bus stop. The temperature outside wasn't friendly. Her quilted jacket was snug, though. The bus stop offered a comfortable bench, where she sat until she could figure out what to do next or where to go.

KimCathy called her phone several times and left voice messages. She thought about going back to the guesthouse, but going back would only make things worse. Mei relaxed on the bench for few hours.

The evening approached quickly. Mei was hungry. A gray SUV slowed down in front of the bus stop.

Alfredo Ivan, a felon in the area, had driven by a couple of times, scoping out Mei. She was awake and looked stranded. Alfredo saw a chance to offer her a ride.

Mei couldn't turn down the offer. She was hungry, and Alfredo was just too nice. Mei got in the front passenger seat.

[Scene 69]

[Inside Alfredo's car]

Alfredo: "Nice to meet you, Mei. What bus are you waiting on?"

Mei: "I don't know."

Alfredo: "Where're you heading?"

Mei: "Nowhere. I'm hungry."

Alfredo: "I have some food in the house. Do you want to come to my house?"

Mei: "Do you live far from here?"

Alfredo: "I live very close by. My place is around the corner from here."

Mei: "Okay."

Alfredo: "I can turn on the heater some more if you want."

Mei: "I'm fine, thanks."

Alfredo had no intention of taking Mei to his place. If Mei hadn't been new to the country, she would have known that the thing around Alfredo's ankle wasn't a smart ankle bracelet. Alfredo was on parole.

[Scene 70]

Ten minutes into the drive, Alfredo pulled into a back alley in a secluded area of an old Bronx neighborhood, the place where he brought all his victims.

He pulled out a knife and ordered Mei to take off her clothes. If she screamed, nothing around there would hear her voice except ghetto rats. Mei hesitated. Alfredo got upset and punched her repeatedly in the face. When the knife started ripping through her jacket, she decided to take it off gently.

Alfredo pinned the blade to her side while abusing her upper body. From her peripheral vision, she saw a pen inside the map pocket of the front passenger's door. She leaned on the door, picked up the pen without Alfredo suspecting, and stabbed him in the cheek. A fight broke out. Mei received a cut on her right arm before forcing her way out of the vehicle. Alfredo tossed Mei's duffle bag out and fled the area.

[Scene 71]

Mei stumbled around the street for some minutes until she fell in front of a house. Mrs. Johnson, a senior citizen relaxing in front of her porch, saw Mei's condition and called an ambulance.

[Scene 72]

Meanwhile, at the community research center in Manhattan,

Mr. Jones's private medical researchers were struggling to accommodate more than a thousand females who wanted to volunteer for what was supposed to be treatment research.

The volunteers were all attracted by the fifty-million-dollar reward. The mayor had made sure there was a doctor present during the interviews to explain the full details about Akar's cure to the people.

The initial population was somewhere around twenty-two thousand females. Approximately twenty-one thousand failed the virginity requirement. Out of the remaining one thousand, only 205 were eighteen years of age or older.

[Scene 73]

Inside the medical research center, volunteer screening was in progress. Bryan and David were some of Mr. Jones's medical researchers. Dr. Terry worked on behalf of the mayor.

A volunteer sat across the table from the three doctors. Bryan was reading out the volunteer's status.

Bryan: "Tamara Tonya. You're nineteen, and your hymen is untouched. You live in Harlem and work in a saloon. Good, that's all I need to know. Dr. Terry, over to you."

Dr. Terry: "Tamara, where are your parents?"

Tamara: "I don't know my father. My mother lives with her boyfriend in downtown Brooklyn. But I'm good. I'm a virgin. I like girls. I'm nineteen, and I'm grown enough to make my own decisions."

Dr. Terry: "All right, Tamara, since you have voluntarily decided to participate, my job is to explain the risk of this research to you."

Tamara: "I'm ready."

Dr. Terry: "Tamara, during this research, you will be required to have sex with a stranger. Do you agree?"

Tamara: "That's not a problem. Shu . . .! For fifty million dollars, I'll have sex with all of you right now."

She smiled.

Dr. Terry: "Good. You probably haven't heard of the Tiamat Stone, so let me explain it to you.
    "The Tiamat Stone carries a dangerous disease, more dangerous than cancer, Ebola, and HIV combined. Anyone who touches the Tiamat Stone will be infected. The victim usually dies in less than a month. During this research, you will be required to touch the Tiamat Stone. Are you willing to do so?"

Tamara: "Me?"

Dr. Terry: "Yeah, you, the volunteer. Do you agree?"

Tamara: "Okay, I'm sure you guys have the cure, right?"

Dr. Terry: "That's why we're here, Tamara. There *is* no cure for the disease except the one we are working on right now. And that's not all. Tamara, have you heard of the inland taipan?"

Tamara: "I've heard of different islands, including the Bahamas. I haven't heard of Taipan."

Dr. Terry: "Inland taipan is not an island resort. Inland taipan is the name of the world's deadliest snake. One drop of venom from this snake is enough to kill one hundred grown men. During this research, you will be required to allow the inland taipan to bite you twice. That's enough venom to kill you in less than ten minutes. Do you understand and agree?"

There was a short silence before Tamara replied.

Tamara: "Oh! Hell no. First you said I'll be required to touch a stone that's deadlier than HIV and Ebola combined. And now you're saying I have to allow myself to get bitten twice by a snake capable of killing a hundred grown men with one bite. How am I supposed to spend the money if I'm dead?"

Bryan: "You are not going to die. The combination of the stone's sickness and the snake's venom is a cure we believe will make you stronger. We've tested it on a virgin rabbit, and it works. The last phase is to test it on a human. That's why we organized this medical research."

Tamara: "This ain't no medical research, men, this is satanic. I'm not a rabbit—I'm a human. What if things don't go the way we plan?"

Bryan: "That's why we're offering fifty million dollars. Tamara, time is against us. We have more volunteers waiting outside. Are you in or out?"

Tamara: "I don't know, men; I have to think about it. Can I use the ladies' room?"

Dr. Terry: "Sure. Walk down the hallway. You'll see the restrooms on your left."

[Scene 74]

On her way to the ladies' room, Tamara took the exit door out of the building. One of the medical guards who saw her while she was running away came to the interview room to report her.

[Scene 75]

[Interview room]

Guard: "Guys, I saw your volunteer running out through the exit door."

David: "Which one of the volunteers?"

Guard: "The one you just interviewed."

David: "Goddamn it."

Bryan: "I'm not surprised. Mr. Terry here did a good job of killing her with his horrendous explanations."

Dr. Terry: "I'm just doing my job."

Bryan: "And I suggest you allow me to do mine. How am I supposed to convince a volunteer that this thing works if you and the mayor intend on making the cure sound like a weapon of mass destruction? Tamara is the eleventh volunteer to walk out of this room and never return, all because of what you told them."

Dr. Terry: "Like I said before we started, my job is not to make your job easier. I'm here by order of the mayor to make sure these volunteers understand the risk involved with your so-called cure."

Bryan: "Well then, would you mind stressing a little more in your speech that we've tested a part of the cure on a rabbit and it works?"

Dr. Terry: "Bryan, if truly you took the same Hippocratic oath I took nineteen years ago when I became a doctor, you should understand that the first priority of a doctor is to save lives."

Bryan: "And as a doctor, I expect you to know that there's always been a risk in every medical invention and cure that man has ever invented. I'm not here because I hate virgins. I'm here to save lives, not to take one."

Dr. Terry: "You're right. You're here to save the life of your rich client's son. I'm here to save millions of innocent lives. Security, please call the next volunteer."

Ana and Maria were the next volunteers. They entered the room and took a seat.

Ana: *"Como estas. Esta es mi hija, Maria. Ella es virgen."*

Bryan: "English. Do either of you speak English?"

Ana: *"Solo un poco. Pero mi hija habla muy bien inglés. Ella es estadounidense."*

Bryan: "Another day in paradise! Dave, do you know anyone who can translate Spanish to English?"

Maria: "I do. 'Just a little, but my daughter speaks very good English. She's an American.' That's what my mother just said in Spanish."

David: "She's here on your behalf?"

Maria: "Yes."

Ana (to Maria): *"Que dijo el? Quiero escuchar todo lo que dice."*
<Translation: "What did he say? I want to hear everything he says.">

Maria: *"Puedes esperar y dejar que terminemos? Ni siquiera sé de qué se trata todo esto."*
<Translation: "Can you wait and let us finish? I don't even know what this is all about.">

Ana: *"Si bajas y te deshaces de esa actitud, estoy seguro de que te explicarán. Entiendes cuánto dinero estamos hablando?* Cincuenta millones de dólares. *"*
<Translation: "If you come down and get rid of that attitude, I'm sure they will explain things to you. Do you understand how much money we are talking about? *Fifty million dollars."*>

Dr. Terry (interrupting): "Maria, I don't understand what you and your mother are saying, but I hope she's not forcing you to participate in this research because of the money."

Maria: "I'm sorry, she's annoying me. No one is forcing me. I chose to participate in the research myself. You can start when you're ready."

Bryan: "All right, Maria. I'm looking at your application here, and you meet all the requirements. You turned eighteen seven months ago, you're a virgin, and you chose to participate voluntarily. Now, Dr. Terry here needs to explain some things to you before you sign the papers, okay?"

Maria: "Okay."

Bryan: "Doctor."

Dr. Terry: "Maria, where is your father?"

Maria: "He lives in El Salvador."

Dr. Terry: "I want to believe your mother is your guardian. So, everything I say, I want you to translate to her in Spanish. During this research, you will be required to copulate with a stranger. Do understand and agree?"

Maria: "That's fine. *Dijo que durante esta investigación, se me exigiría copular con un extraño. Me preguntó si entendía y estaba de acuerdo. No tienes que decir una palabra, ya dije que sí.* Continue."

Terry: "What I'm about to explain next has been tested on a virgin rabbit, and it works fine. Therefore, I don't want you to panic. There's a stone called the Tiamat Stone. The stone has a long history, but what you need to know is that anyone who touches it will be infected. This infection is so powerful that it will kill the victim in less than thirty days unless the victim completes the treatment process."

Ana: *"Que dijo el?"*
<Translation:"What did he say?">

Maria: *"No sé qué diablos está diciendo este tipo. Te lo explicaré cuando termine de hablar."*
<Translation: "I don't know what the hell this guy is saying. I'll explain to you when he finished talking.">
"What is the remaining treatment process?"

Dr. Terry: "The last process in the research is a cure for the Tiamat infection. After you have been infected by the Tiamat disease, you will have to allow an inland taipan, a very deadly snake, to bite you twice for the Tiamat sickness to be cured in you. And then, for you to be eligible for the fifty-million-dollar reward, you will be required to have sex with a stranger who is also carrying the Tiamat disease. Do you understand and agree?"

Maria: "All right, hold on a second. *Lo que este idiota me pide que haga es peor que regañar a Pablo Escobar. Primero dijo que tendrían que infectarme con una enfermedad mortal, y luego una serpiente mortal me debe morder dos veces para iniciar una cura. Después de eso, debo tener relaciones sexuales con una persona que porta una enfermedad mortal antes de que pueda obtener el dinero."*
<Translation: "What this idiot is asking me to do is worse than snitching on Pablo Escobar. First, he said they would have to infect me with a deadly disease, and then a deadly snake must bite me twice to initiate a cure. After that, I must have sex with a person carrying a deadly disease before I can get the money.">

Ana: *"Serpiente mortal? Están locos? En el momento en que vi a este gilipollas con un bigote de cabra, supe que no estaba haciendo nada bueno."*
<Translation: "Deadly snake? Are they insane? The moment I saw this asshole with a goat mustache, I knew he was up to nothing good.">

Maria: *"Dijo que lo probaron con un conejo virgen y funciona."*
<Translation: "He said they've tested the cure on a virgin rabbit and it works.">

Ana: *"Nos vemos como conejos? Si el experimento es seguro, por qué no pueden probarlo con sus propias hijas? María, encuéntrame en el auto ahora o te mataré yo mismo."*
<Translation: "Do we look like rabbits? If the experiment is safe, why can't they test it on their own daughters? Maria, meet me in the car now, or else I'll kill you myself.">

Ana and Maria walked out of the inter-view. None of the doctors understood the last words Maria and her mother had said.

Failure was frustrating, yet the hopeless interview process continued throughout the night. One after another, they interviewed more than two hundred volunteers. In the end, the results were always the same: the volunteer either walked out of the room or promised to return the following week.

[Scene 76]

While the search for a virgin female went on in Manhattan, Mr. Jones was in Egypt doing his own research on the Tiamat Stone.

Macarthur Obasi, one of Egypt's great wise men, led Mr. Jones to the Alexandria reserve where the Tiamat Stone had first come to light in Egypt.

The first Egyptian marine divers who'd found it in the mid-thirties had initially been looking for the Ptolemaic city of Alexandria underwater. The power of the stone was soon discovered after everyone who touched it died of the same illness in less than a month.

Before the Tiamat Stone claimed its last victim in Egypt, an Egyptian archeologist reading an ancient book written by an unknown pharaoh discovered the story and cure.

Valencia Gail, the daughter of the victim, was the first virgin to try the Tiamat cure. The cure worked as the pharaoh had predicted in his book; however, Valencia died of a strange sickness two months after she volunteered for the cure. The remaining part of the book, which had been missing, was later found in the early sixties. It revealed why Valencia had died.

The volunteer could not be of the same blood as the victim, and as opposed to Akar's cure, which had been written in the early forties, the virgin, after having sex with the victim, could not have sex with another person again except the victim, or else he or she would die.

It seemed as if the more Mr. Jones dug into this thing, the more complicated it got. It was already proving impossible to find a woman to volunteer for what sounded like a suicide mission. Perhaps, if the price were right, one might eventually find a mentally deficient person to volunteer. But where on earth would you find a woman who would accept not having sex again for the rest of her natural life because she participated in one unreasonable medical research project?

Mr. Jones was a mathematician who'd become a businessman. If Jason's problem had been algebra, Mr. Jones would have solved it himself.

A lack of belief in things like the Akar cure filled him with doubt. However, despite his skepticism, he couldn't dispute the effect of the Tiamat Stone. He had seen it with his own eyes. Whether he believed in the cure or not, it was the only hope Jason had of surviving.

Mr. Jones had traveled to Egypt in search of answers. What he brought back to the United States was more than what his medical research team could handle.

[Scene 77]

The private jet carrying Mr. Jones touched down at JFK around 8 p.m.

[Scene 78]

Bryan was waiting at the airport to give Mr. Jones some good news. It seemed, at long last, after six days of round-the-clock interviews, they'd finally found a virgin who was willing to take the risk. Little did Bryan know that the cure had just taken a new turn.

[Scene 79]

At the Jones residence in Manhattan, Bryan and David discussed the new information that Mr. Jones had brought back from Egypt. They were glad to hear that at least a human had tried the cure in the past and that it had worked. The new problem they faced was how to inform the two female volunteers about the new discovery. For fifty million dollars, anyone could promise not to have sex again forever. But keeping such a promise was highly improbable. No reasonable lawyer would advise his client to sign such an agreement.

   With the new discovery, it was very unlikely that Dr. Terry would be willing to participate. If Bryan and David proceeded without explaining the risk, they could lose their medical licenses and possibly face jail sentences.

   Their medical conscience beat faster than their hearts. Mr. Jones didn't have a medical conscience; he believed money was the answer to all concerns. Thus, his offer went from fifty million dollars to a staggering one hundred million dollars.

[Scene 80]

The next day, Bryan and David were only expecting two volunteers to report at the research center. Instead, over forty-five thousand females showed up. Bryan had to cancel the interviews. The majority of the females weren't virgins. Most of them had come because of the money.

   Bryan waited seven hours at his office for the two virgin

volunteers who'd promise to come back. It was now past 8 p.m. If the two ladies were still willing to participate, they should have arrived at the office before eight.

Dave stayed in the research center lobby in case any of the previous volunteers had changed their mind. At exactly 8:30 p.m. on the dot, Bryan grabbed his vintage bag, closed the office door, and headed to the parking lot.

[Scene 81]

Nicole Peoples, a homeless virgin Bryan had been waiting for, had been sitting on the curb the whole time waiting for the doctors to arrive. She was wearing the same gray winter jacket she'd worn the day before. Her arms were wrapped around her knees. She appeared to be sleeping where she sat.

[Scene 82]

Bryan felt compassion for Nicole. He took her to the nearest motel and gave her enough money to get a room for a week.

[Scene 83]

[Brooklyn Hospital]

The curtain swung open. Nurse Shane had brought Mei's prescription papers. Since Mei had arrived at the hospital, she hadn't spoken a word. Eleven stitches had been used to close the cut on her right arm. She was scheduled to leave the emergency room the next morning.

Nurse Shane asked if Mei knew who had attacked her. Mei shook her head.

Mei hadn't been raped. Doctors had confirmed her hymen was still present. But her clothes and face had shown signs of sexual assaults. Police officers from the county would be returning later to ask Mei a few questions. She waited until Nurse Shane left the room. Emergency room areas are often busy, so Mei used the opportunity to walk out of the hospital unnoticed.

[Scene 84]

Mei passed the night at the nearest twenty-four-hour restaurant.

[Scene 85]

In the morning, Mei wrote a note to Jason and another one to her parents in China. Her plan was to mail the notes at the nearest post office when it opened.

[Two hours later, at the restaurant]

Mei couldn't move her body. The slice of apple she'd eaten at the hospital was all she'd had in two days. Her body was weak. She collapsed on the floor with the notes in her hand. A few seconds passed before someone noticed her and called the ambulance.

[Mei's note to her parents in China]

"我們上次發言已經有一段時間了,一切順利.我抵達這一個星期後，我在紐約市的一所昂貴的房子裡找到了一份工作。當我節省足夠的錢，我會給你一個好的手機，所以我們可以永遠保持聯繫。我愛你，每一天過去，我都想念你們。我對大家的問候美陳。"
<Translation: It has been a while since we last spoke. I hope all is well. A week after I arrived here, I got a job as a maid in an expensive house in New York City. When I save enough money, I'll send you a nice phone so that we can always keep in touch. I love you, and with each day that passes, I miss you all. My regards to everyone. Mei Chan.">

[Mei's note to Jason]

"I wish I could deliver the words in this note to you in person. Hopefully, if you are reading it, I want you to know I wrote it in tears from the bottom my heart.

"I never knew what love really felt like until I met you. My mind was closed, but you found your way in. You filled my mind with love, locked the door, and took away the key.

"Now it doesn't matter how far apart we are. You are always on my mind. Even when I sleep, I see you in my dreams.

"Since that evening when we separated, life and everyone has been mean to me. I don't know where to go from here. I hope you get better soon, and if God is willing, I'll see you again one day. If not, I wish you the best in life. Mei Chan."

[Scene 86]

Eleven days had passed since Jason had touched the Tiamat Stone. Life support was the only thing keeping him alive at the Reno State Hospital. Doctors gave him less than two weeks to live.

[Scene 87]

On the morning of November 3, Dr. Bryan received a call at his office.

One of the nurses who worked with Bryan told him of a homeless lady at the hospital who was willing to volunteer for the Akar cure. Bryan's first thought was that it was Nicole Peoples, that she must have come to the hospital looking for him.

Bryan believed Nicole was a young teenager who'd run away from home. Bryan had a teenage daughter who resembled Nicole. He wouldn't allow Nicole to go through such a predicament. However, he sent seven hundred dollars and a note to the lady he assumed was Nicole.

[Scene 88]

When Mei received the envelope, she didn't understand why it had been sent to her.

Bryan told the nurses to escort her from the hospital and tell her not to return except when she needed treatment.

Nurse Tina had dealt with a lot of greedy volunteers at the hospital, so she believed Mei was just another one of them. Plus, at the hospital, Mei had only been diagnosed with hunger after the ambulance had brought her there.

Mei read the note after Nurse Tina led her off the property. It read: "Hello, Nicole. I'm sorry I couldn't see you today. I was very busy. However, after considering your application, we've decided not to make you a participant in our ongoing medical research due to your age. Please kindly accept the token we've sent you as compensation for your time. Thanks. Bryan White."

Mei didn't know Bryan White or why he referred to her as Nicole. Nevertheless, Mei knew what to do with the money. At the first store she came to, she bought some food, a jacket, and a backpack. By then, she was tired of running. Early November had been unusually cold in New York. After a week of suffering, she had finally come to the realization that even though life in New York seemed better than life in Boluo, there was no place like home. But Mei had one last thing to do before going back to China.

[Scene 89]

Outside the Chinese restaurant where Mei had eaten her first reasonable lunch in days, she flagged a cab. She told the driver to take her to Letch Park. She still had a black eye from Alfredo's punches. From the way she looked, the driver wasn't sure if Mei had transport fare.

If Mei had been a native, she would have known not to show a bunch of fifties to a cab driver in New York City. To make matters worse, Mei told the driver she didn't know how to get to her destination, the only secret no passenger should ever tell a taxi driver in America.

[Scene 90]

Alonzo, a fifteen-year taxi veteran in New York, used the opportunity to maximize profit. They took off around 6:15 p.m. and arrived at Letch Park around 6:40 p.m. The taxi parked in the same spot where Jason had parked the first time he and Mei had come there.

Alonzo: "Is this where you want me to drop you?"

Mei: "Yes."

Alonzo: "It's getting dark. What have you come to do in Letch Park at this time of the day?"

Mei: "I left something here a few days ago. I'll be back in less than ten minutes."

Alonzo: "You want me to wait for you?"

Mei: "Yes, I won't take too long."

Alonzo: "It's not about time, ma'am, it's about money. You already owe sixty-five dollars. Every additional minute will cost you three dollars. Pay me what you owe first before you leave."

Mei: "No problem."

Mei paid sixty-five bucks. Alonzo gave Mei a flashlight and waited on the roadside.

[Scene 91]

This time, Mei was alone. She scrambled through the woods with Alonzo's flashlight, using her past memory to navigate her path. The abandoned house needed no description; it was the only building in the isolated east part of Letch Park.

[Scene 92]

The moment the house appeared in sight, Mei ran inside and cautiously searched for the Tiamat Stone.

She knew the danger of touching the stone, which was why she'd bought a backpack. She wouldn't be using the backpack that evening, though. It was apparent that someone had removed the stone. She turned the flashlight in the direction of the table where Jason had kissed her and gazed at the little pyramid for a moment.

A wolf spider ran across the table. Startled, Mei dropped the flashlight, and it flickered. She picked it up and ran back to the cab.

CATAPHRASE D

"A person who wakes up in the middle of
nowhere is stranded. A lost person is
one who doesn't know where his
life is going."

—Teni A.

[Scene 93]

[Inside the cab]

Alonzo: "What took you so long? I was about to leave when I saw you coming. What happened?"

Mei: "Nothing. Here is your flashlight. Let's go."

Alonzo: "Go where?"

Mei: "Take me to the nearest beach."

Alonzo: "Beach?"

Mei: "Yes, beach."

Alonzo searched his navigation map.

Alonzo: "The nearest one is Brighton Beach. Is that where you want to go?"

Mei: "Yes."

Alonzo: "All right."

Alonzo got back on the road.

Alonzo: "You forgot something at the beach, too?"

Mei: "No."

Alonzo: "Do you work night shift at the beach?"

Mei: "No, why did you ask?"

Alonzo: "You are the only person I've seen going to parks and beaches at this time of the day.

"I can tell you are from China. I work at the airport on weekends. I pick up a lot of Chinese tourists coming to the state for the first time. First-time arrivals are always unusual. One night, around 11 p.m. at JFK Airport, an Asian lady who'd just arrived from Hong Kong asked me to take her to 9/11. I said, '*Where?*' She said, '9/11, 9/11.' I asked, 'You mean the Twin Towers memorial?' She replied, 'Yes, 9/11.'

"I took her there, and after she finished taking pictures, guess where she wants me to take her next."

Mei: "Where?"

Alonzo: "Central Park Zoo. I said. 'What, you're going there to spend the night with the lions?'

Alonzo laughed before he continued speaking.

"Man, you guys are very funny. But I like Asian people. They are very nice. Especially Chinese people. They are good tippers.

So, Mei, are you also going to the beach to take pictures?"

Mei: "No. I need to do something for someone I love before I leave the country."

Alonzo: "Okay, okay. He's waiting for you at the beach?"

Mei: "Who?"

Alonzo: "The person you love."

Mei: "No, he's at the hospital."

Alonzo: "He works at the hospital, or he's receiving treatment at the hospital?"

Mei: "He's receiving treatment."

Alonzo: "I'm sorry to hear that. I hope he gets well."

Mei: "Can I ask you a question?"

Alonzo: "Sure."

Mei: "Do you think it's wise to risk your life for someone you love even if the person's mother doesn't like you?"

Alonzo: "If the person is your spouse and as long as the person loves you, what his mother thinks about you doesn't matter. So, I would say there's nothing wrong if you do what you would do for your child for your spouse."

Mei: "What if the person is not a spouse? Let's say the person is your boyfriend or girlfriend."

Alonzo: "Then you have to be really crazy in love to risk your life for a friend."

[Scene 94]

Around 8:40 p.m., Alonzo dropped Mei off at Brighton Resort. From there, Mei walked to the ocean shore.

[Scene 95]

Darkness had finally taken over the day. No one was at the beach when Mei got there. She sat on the shore and watched how the full moon brightened the ocean's surface. The gentle waves swept up to her feet where she sat. Gradually, the clapping sound of the water filled Mei with dread and loneliness. The presence of darkness around the beach brought anxiety, but the brightness of the moon overcame the fear that lurked within the night.

After Mei spent an hour admiring the blissful sight of nature, she stood up and removed all her clothes. Once nude, she stepped a couple of feet into the water.

As nature is one of man's best friends, it can also be man's worst enemy. Some of the world's most dangerous predators live in the ocean, and people often say they come to the shore at night to feed. Mei shivered in fear as she recited the beautiful princess chant.

> *"I send the power*
> *of the wind to you,*
> *Mzui, beautiful*
> *princess of the salty*
> *ocean.*
> *I summon you from*
> *your dwelling place.*
> *In the name of Raphael,*
> *Rohi, and Rehoba,*
> *arise.*
> *Bring me the*
> *beauty of Nymph*
> *and the healing of*
> *Nodens. Take me to*
> *the land beneath the*
> *ocean. Show me the*
> *four dreams of Amzirhote.*
> *Samna El Abastani."*

Mei felt the ocean wind drawing her in as she rapidly became unconscious. She crawled out of the water naked and fell on the bank.

The wind over the ocean grew stronger and closer. Every bit of sound around the beach slowly faded away.

[Scene 96]

Mei found herself sitting on a dune in the middle of a hybrid island. One part of the island behind her was a sea, and over the sea, the full moon shone brighter. The sun shone over the remaining part of the island.

The moon over the sea suddenly moved downwards towards the water, gradually changing shape until it became a huge white horse and came out of the sea.

Xuxi, Zion, and Orion, three beautiful crystal mermaids, accompanied the horse. Each of them was carrying a golden basket full of all sorts of colored diamonds. The white horse and the three mermaids presented themselves and the treasure in front of Mei.

Behind Mei, darkness appeared. She looked back and saw the sun coming down while changing shape at the same time. The sun became a huge yellow horse, which ran across the island towards Mei. Trailing behind the yellow horse were a thousand soundless golden honeybees. They too presented themselves to Mei. The diamonds and the bees lit up the entire island in magnificent multicolor.

Xuxi had the ability to read minds. Mei wouldn't accept their offer; she was hungry.

Zion had the ability to change anything. With a touch, she turned the diamonds in her golden basket to apples. Mei wouldn't eat; she was cold.

Orion had the power to conjure fire. With a touch, she turned the diamonds in her golden basket into a furnace.

The yellow horse switched her tail, and the thousand golden bees around her started to sing. Perhaps a sweet melody would change Mei's mind. Mei didn't show any sign of interest.

In the twinkling of an eye, everything around Mei vanished. The horses, mermaids, bees, diamonds, apples, ocean, and desert—everything disappeared without a trace. Mei was left in total darkness.

Everywhere was dark and silent. Something watery touched Mei's hair. For a second, a stroke of lightning brightened the sky, and then a heavy rain started to fall. Shortly, the rain stopped, and the sun rose steadily.

When Mei rose, she was alone in a forest.

[Scene 97]

As she walked between the trees, she saw a thin fog about forty yards away. She looked closely in the direction of the fog and saw a cabin looming in the distance.

She ran towards the cabin. When she got closer, she saw an old brown-skinned man sitting on the floor in front of it, banging a goblet drum. The old man appeared to be blind. He repeated, "Maveth, maveth . . . ," while his face focused in one direction.

Mei didn't get a response from the old man after several greetings. The sound of a crying child broke out in the cabin. Mei proceeded to the entrance.

[Scene 98]

The cabin's interior reflected green light, except for one room where white rays of light broke through a partially open door. Mei skulked towards the white light. When she opened the door, she saw that the old man who had been sitting outside was now standing in the center of the room. The white light inside the room was coming from the old man's body. Mei flinched and ran out.

[Scene 99]

Outside the cabin, the forest had changed to a desert. Mei stepped out of the cabin, baffled.

    After moving a couple of steps away from the cabin, she looked back and saw a huge pyramid where the cabin had once stood.

From behind, a hand clapped Mei on the shoulder. Another brown-skinned man wearing a loincloth greeted Mei in Arabic. He gestured to the camel, as if to offer Mei a ride. She looked at the camel but didn't say a word.

    He offered Mei water from his calcite jug. She shook her head. He spoke more Arabic that Mei didn't understand and then rode away on his camel.

    In the direction he went, a sandstorm brewed. Mei tried to escape the storm's rage, but she couldn't make her feet move as fast as she wanted them to. Her legs quivered as she tried to move faster. The sandstorm moved closer, growing wider and stronger until Mei was engulfed in the sand.

[Scene 100]

The storm was over. A barking sounded continuously. Mei

coughed and cleaned the dust off her face.

When the dust finally cleared from her eyes, she was alone on an empty street. The barking sound continued. Mei got up and traced the sound to a park nearby.

[Scene 101]

At the center of the park, a white dog nervously barked at meat on a grill.

A lone swing moved back and forth on the playground beside the dog. Just as Mei was about to take the meat and toss it to the dog, a black crow grabbed the meat and flew away.

Woman's voice: "You seem to be lost."

Mei turned around and saw a tall, gorgeous woman wearing a glassy blue crown and a shiny, elegant blue sequined mermaid dress.

Mei: "Who are you?"

Woman: "Who I am is not important. That's not why you came here. Why did you send Boreas to my dwelling place?"

Mei: "I don't know you. I didn't send anyone to you."

The woman moved closer to Mei, walking around her in a circle as she spoke.

Woman: "You did. I'm amazed you forget so quickly. When a human's mind gets pregnant with thoughts, their mouth gives birth to them as words. The words will then go out and search for where to dwell.

"Young lady, where you are standing is where words become living beings, a place where thoughts are born.

"Look around you and you will notice that everything you've seen so far is what you have once said or thought in your mind. The things you don't recognize are either the words that have grown bigger since you delivered them with your mouth or the meaningless ones you once spoke."

Mei: "I don't recognize you."

Woman: "Then why did you send Boreas to wake me up?"

Mei: "Who is Boreas?"

Woman: "The god of the wind."

Just then, and despite her fright, Mei remembered something.

Mei: "The chant?"

Woman: "Yes."

Mei: "Mzui?"

Woman: "Yes, I'm Mzui. Why did you summon me?"

Mei desperately tried to speak, but the words wouldn't come out. She could hear Mzui talking. At the same time, she heard the long wail of a siren.

[Scene 102]

Two paramedics were standing over Mei, pressing her stomach. She woke up on a stretcher at Brighton Beach around 9 a.m.

Two paramedics were trying to resuscitate her.

Paramedic 1: "She's awake."

Paramedic 2: "She doesn't look like she got washed up on the shore."

Paramedic 1: "Why is she naked?"

Paramedic 2: "Get her clothes. Can I have an oxygen mask, please? Ma'am, just relax. I've got you."

Mei: "I'm fine."

Paramedic 2: "I know. Just relax. I'm going to cover you with this blanket. Your clothes are wet."

Mei: "I want my clothes. I have to leave now."

Paramedic 2: "Did someone bring you here? Did anyone

attack you? How did you get here?"

Mei: "I'm fine. No one attacked me. I slept here last night."

Paramedic 2: "Naked?"

Mei: "Yes."

Paramedic 2: "Are you sure you don't want a doctor to check you? Your body temperature is very low; you could be suffering from hypothermia."

Mei remained silent. Her body was shaking.

Paramedic 1: "Ma'am, where do you live?"

Mei: "Manhattan."

Paramedic 1: "All right, I'm going to take you to the ambulance so you can get some heat before you leave. Okay?"

[Scene 103]

When she was done warming up in the ambulance, one of the paramedics handed Mei her backpack and her partially dried clothes.

Mei checked her backpack for what was left of her seven hundred dollars. She still had three hundred dollars and some change left.

[Scene 104]

Breakfast started at 10 a.m. at the oceanside cafeteria near the beach.

Mei waited thirty minutes for the cafeteria to open. During that time, she reminisced on her dreams. She had never dreamed that much in one night. She could barely remember some of the dreams. The last one was still fresh in her memory, though. She could see Mzui's face in her imagination, just as she'd seen it in the dream.

The open sign on the cafeteria door came on. A few people were already in line. Mei didn't notice them until she looked in the direction of the door.

One female Caucasian senior citizen stared at Mei as if she hadn't seen an Asian woman before. Perhaps, after Mei's sleep on the beach, her face needed to be cleaned off.

[Scene 105]

Mei headed to the ladies' room to clean the early morning sleep out of her eyes and to wash her face.

Another woman was exiting the ladies' room as Mei was entering.

Woman: "Wow, that's cute."

Mei wasn't surprised. It wasn't the first time a lady had given her a sexual compliment.

[Scene 106]

Halfway into the restroom, Mei saw her reflection in the mirror over the pedestal sink.

Something in her eyes was lustrous. Both of her eyeballs were emitting a slight glamorous blue light. She washed her face multiple times to see if that cleared away the glow, but nothing changed. The blue light was still there. Now she understood why the old lady at the door had been staring at her. Carefully, she walked out of the ladies' room and exited the cafeteria without drawing attention to herself.

[Scene 107]

Various resort activities around Brighton Beach opened at 10:30 a.m. Joshline Price, a Brighton native who owned a store in the neighborhood, had just opened her shop when Mei showed up at the register with her blue eyes.

At first, Joshline didn't notice Mei's eyes, as she was facing the shelf behind the checkout register.

Joshline: "Give me a second, ma'am; I'll attend to you shortly."

Mei did not respond, so Joshline stepped down from the stepladder and faced the register.

Joshline: "Good morning. Wow, those are nice Acuvue lenses you've got there. How did you make them shine?"

Mei: "To be honest, ma'am, I don't know how they got there. In which aisle can I find sunglasses?"

Joshline: "Sunglasses are behind you."

Mei: "Oh, thanks."

Joshline: "You're welcome."

When Mei was done paying for her glasses, she asked Joshline how to get to the nearest bus stop. Joshline gave her directions and a copy of a Brighton city metro map. She wanted to talk more about Mei's eyes, but Mei was in a hurry.

According to Akar's cure, after the virgin has seen the blue princess, the next step is to get bitten by a snake. Mei didn't know anywhere in New York City where she could find an inland taipan. The lady at the register seemed to be interested in weird things, though. It was possible she might know where one could buy a snake. Mei turned back to the register on her way out of the store.

Mei: "Excuse me."

Joshline: "Hey, you're back. What can I do for you?"

Mei: "Yes, I was wondering if you knew where I can buy a snake."

Joshline: "I'm sorry, you said a snake?"

Mei: "Yes."

Joshline: "No . . . I'm sorry. But I know a guy who might be able to help you. Do you know where the Crab Craving restaurant is?"

Mei: "No, I'm not from this area."

Joshline: "That's fine. Go out of here and make a left. Matter of fact, did you see a Brighton Inn hotel on your way here?"

Mei: "The one along the road, before one gets here?"

Joshline: "Yeah, it's the only hotel before you get to Brighton Beach. Go there and ask for Ken. His last name is Roy. He works at the Crab Craving restaurant inside the hotel. He does a lot of farming and fishing. Often, when he catches things like tarantulas, water snakes, or colored fish, he comes around here to sell them. He sold a cute white rabbit to my sister, very cute."

Mei: "He works at the restaurant in the hotel?"

Joshline: "Yep. Just go there and ask for Ken. Everybody there knows him."

Mei: "Thanks for your help."

Joshline: "No problem. Take care."

Other than farming and fishing, Ken also surfed. He'd

come from Virginia to New York for better job opportunities. His uncle owned a small business that supplied crabs to local restaurants in Brighton. Occasionally, during his days off from Crab Craving, he would join his uncle on Sheepshead Bay for crab fishing.

[Scene 108]

It was around 2 p.m. when Mei met with Ken at the Brighton Inn hotel. They met outside the restaurant within the hotel premises. Mei had her sunglasses on.

Ken: "Sorry to keep you waiting. I don't think I've seen your face before. I'm Ken. You wanted to see me?"

Mei: "Yes, sorry to bother you. I'm Mei. Someone referred me to you."

Ken: "I don't teach surfing anymore, if that's why you came. I can refer you to a friend who still does it if you want. He's a very good wave rider, just like me."

Mei: "No thanks. I came to see you for something different. I want to buy a snake."

Ken: "A snake?"

Mei: "Yes."

Ken: "What's your name again?"

Mei: "Mei Chan."

Ken: "Who told you to come see me?"

Mei: "A lady who works at the Mossy store."

Ken: "Joshline?"

Mei: "I don't remember her name."

Ken: "She's chubby? She has long blonde hair like yours?"

Mei: "Yes."

Ken: "Yeah, that's Joshline. I sold a little rabbit to her sister. Okay, I can help you with that. I caught a milk snake and a cottonmouth last weekend, but someone already paid for them. The person should be picking them up today.

"I'll be going to the bay tomorrow, though. I should be able to get you a queen snake. I have a painted turtle at home if you are interested; I can get you that one today."

Mei: "I want a different type of snake. How fast do you think you can get me an inland taipan?"

Ken: "Inland taipan?"

Mei: "Yes."

Ken: "If you're looking for a pet snake, I wouldn't advise getting that kind of snake. I mean, unless you are planning a suicide by snake, you shouldn't put a taipan in your house."

Mei: "I understand, but that's what I want. Can you get one for me?"

Ken: "Inland taipans are not found in North America; they have to be brought into the country. I know a guy in Virginia who keeps various venomous snakes. I doubt if he has a taipan. However, I can't tell for sure what he has or what he doesn't have unless I speak to him."

Mei: "How soon can you get in touch with him?"

Ken: "How much are you willing to pay for the taipan?"

Mei: "Two hundred dollars."

Ken: "He's gonna want more than that. For that kind of snake, he won't charge anything less than a thousand."

Mei: "Okay."

Ken: "You have a thousand?"

Mei: "Yes."

Ken: "Perfect. Like I said, I have to talk to him first to see if he has what you want. So, give me your number. I'll contact you as soon as I get in touch with him."

Mei: "I'm not going anywhere. I'll wait for you in the lobby."

Ken: "I haven't spoken to the guy since I left Virginia. In fact, I don't even have his number. I have to call a friend who has his number to contact him. Moreover, I just finished my shift. I was on my way home when I got your call."

Mei: "How much do you want to sell that painted turtle for?"

Ken: "Fifty bucks. It's a baby painted turtle."

Mei reached into her bag, brought out a new fifty-dollar bill, and gave it to Ken.

Mei: "You can keep that fifty and the turtle. I want you to call your friend in Virginia now."

Ken: "All right, I can make that work. Give me a minute."

Ken stepped to the side and called his friend in Virginia.

[A minute later]

Ken: "I just spoke to my friend. I told him to call the guy and ask if he has an inland taipan for sale. He'll call me back in five minutes."

Mei: "That's fine. I'll wait."

Ken: "Let's go to the lobby. Where do you work?"

Mei: "I don't have a job."

Ken: "I understand. Rich dad, rich mom, the house is always a bore. Sometimes, you just wish you had a pet to play with. You shouldn't play with the taipan, though; it's not a nice pet. I can get you a cute little puppy if you don't mind. Do you like dogs?"

Mei: "Yes. No. Yes. Don't worry about a puppy. Just get me a taipan."

Ken: "Taipan. I got you."

[Scene 109]

Shortly after they arrived at the hotel lobby, Ken's phone rang. He stepped to the side again to answer the call.

[A minute later]

Ken: "All right, Mei, here's the deal. The guy doesn't have an inland taipan, but he knows where he can get one. He's going to charge an extra two hundred dollars if you want him to bring the snake from Virginia to New York. Otherwise, you'll have to travel to Virginia if all you want to pay is a thousand. Which one do you prefer?"

Mei: "I'll go to Virginia."

Ken: "When?"

Mei: "Today, maybe tomorrow."

Ken: "Great. Let me give you his number. His name is Paul Huge. Call him when you get to Richmond. Tell him Ken Roy sent you."

Mei jotted down the number.

Mei: "Thanks."

Ken: "No problem, anytime. Hey, be careful with that snake, and here is my number. Let me know if you need anything else."

Ken saw Mei as a rich kid wanting to buy an exotic pet. Mei, however, after persuading him with fifty bucks, only had 330 dollars left on her.

[Scene 110]

There was a small room in the lobby area where guests could use free Internet on the hotel's computer. Mei got on the Internet and searched for the next bus leaving from Brooklyn to Richmond, Virginia.

She found a seat on a Canyon bus traveling from Brooklyn to Virginia at 8 p.m. that evening. Plus taxes, she would pay $49.99 cash before boarding the bus. The return-trip ticket for noon the next day would cost her another fifty-one dollars plus taxes.

[Scene 111]

With just a backpack and 230 dollars in her pocket, Mei arrived in Richmond a little after 2 a.m.

The bus station where she alighted was scanty. The few people who got off the bus with Mei left soon after. The Tuesday morning was cold. Mei looked for the nearest pay phone and gave Paul a call.

[Scene 112]

Paul was a forty-two-year-old divorced zoologist who had a passion for collecting cats and venomous snakes. He lived alone in a three-bedroom house in Richmond. He was about to go to bed when his phone rang. Mei introduced herself and mentioned her referrer, Ken Roy. Paul hadn't been able to find a fully-grown taipan; however, he had been able to get a nine-month-old, thirty-inch inland taipan. Thus, he would only charge Mei seven hundred dollars.

He told Mei to meet him at the nearest Starbucks from the bus station at 9 a.m. Mei had another thought in mind.

Mei (on the phone): "Can I spend the night at your place, if you don't mind? I couldn't find a hotel, and I need to take a shower."

Mei's voice was attractive, and other than twenty-two venomous snakes and four cats, Paul was alone in the house. It was a request he couldn't refuse.

Paul (on the phone):"Sure. I'll be at the station in twenty minutes."

[Scene 113]

Different thoughts ran through Paul's mind as he put his living room in order. The room where he would accommodate Mei hadn't been used in a while. He made sure the room's bathroom and carpet were clean before he drove to Allen Station to pick Mei up.

[Scene 114]

[Allen Bus Station]

When Paul laid eyes on Mei at the station, she was just as attractive as her voice had sounded on the phone.

[Scene 115]

Paul made no attempt to hide his feelings. He told Mei how beautiful she looked the moment she entered his car. Adding to Paul's desire, Mei took off her jacket and glasses and gave him a thank-you hug.

Paul had never seen anything like Mei's eyes before. They were illuminated, like those of a cat in a dark room. Hers were even stranger, as they emitted a slight blue light. He asked if she had eye implants. Mei shook her head.

Paul couldn't take his eyes off the skimpy pink lace of her bra. Throughout the twenty-minute trip to Paul's house, he didn't remember to talk about the snake or anything related to it. Mei's beauty took the conversation in another direction.

[Scene 116]

They arrived at Paul's house on Vincent Street around 3:47 a.m. The motion sensor light in the driveway came on. The neighborhood was silent.

Mei stepped out of the car and waited for Paul to lead the way.

Paul: "Are you cold?"

Mei: "A little bit."

Paul: "Don't worry, I left the heater on before I left the house."

Mei could see a cat prowling in the window as they walked to the front door.

Mei: "You have a cat?"

Paul (smiling): "Yes, a couple of them, and some snakes. Are you afraid of cats?"

Mei: "No, I like cats."

Paul: "My cats are very friendly, especially Poke. He should be at the entrance when I open the door."

[Scene 117]

Poke was at the entrance, just like Paul had said, when the door was opened.

The cat suddenly freaked out and ran away when he saw Mei's blue eyes.

Paul: "That was weird. Cats only behave that way when they see something strange. You can come in. It's all right. He was just hungry."

Mei: "Where is the snake?"

Paul: "It's in the basement. I keep all my snakes in the basement."

Mei: "You have more than one snake?"

Paul: "Yes, that's what I do mostly. I collect all kinds of venomous snakes, breed them, and sell their venom. Do you want to see the taipan first before you take a shower?"

Mei: "Yes."

Paul: "All right, follow me to the basement. Be careful not to touch any of the cages. A bite from any of the snakes down there will kill you within three hours. Especially the one you requested."

The conversation continued on the way to the basement.

Mei: "Have you ever been bitten by any of the snakes?"

Paul: "Oh yeah, a couple of times. The good thing is I have the anti-venom of every species I have in this house—except for the inland taipan."

[Scene 118]

[In the basement]

Paul: "About two months ago, I got bitten by this bad boy right here."

Mei: "The cobra?"

Paul: "Yep. Even though he's known me for two years, he bit me like I was a stranger. That's your snake right there on the left."

Mei: "It's beautiful."

Paul: "Yes, it is. That's why I call it the golden devil. A bite from that snake will kill you in less than forty minutes. Do you mind if I ask why you specifically requested an inland taipan? I've been collecting and selling snakes for almost ten years, and this is the first time anyone has ever requested one."

Mei: "If I tell you why I need it, you won't believe me. So, let's just say I want to keep it as a pet."

Paul: "It's all good. I understand. The majority of my clients buy snakes for different reasons. Come with me upstairs. Let me show you the shower and the guest room."

Mei: "Thanks."

[Scene 119]

[Thirty minutes later]

Paul was relaxing in the living room while Mei was upstairs in the guest room. He was halfway asleep when he heard the sound of Poke clomping down the stairs to the kitchen.

[Scene 120]

Paul looked in the direction of the stairs, and Mei was standing on the steps in her pink underwear and a skirt. Her blue eyes radiated an unspeakable beauty. For a moment, they both looked at each other.

Mei: "Do you have a towel I can use?"

Paul: "Yeah, yeah, I have one upstairs. Let me get it for you."

[Scene 121]

The last thing Paul thought Mei would ask for prior to picking her up was a towel. The only towel he had was still hanging somewhere in the bathroom, slightly wet. He plucked the towel from a rack, feeling it with his face along the way to the living room.

[Scene 122]

[In the living room]

Paul: "See if you can use this one."

Mei: "Thanks. I'll bring it back when I'm done."

Paul: "No problem."

Paul sat back on the living room couch, searching the channels for something to keep him entertained until Mei returned. Half an hour later, Mei returned to the living room wearing the towel. She sat on another couch across from Paul.

Mei: "Paul, there's something I want to tell you."

Paul: "I'm listening."

Mei: "I only have two hundred dollars to pay for the snake. But I can make up for the rest."

Paul: "How?"

Mei: "I can dance. Do you like dancing?"

Paul: "Yeah, I do. But I'm going to want more. I mean, two hundred dollars is way too little compared to what I told you I was going to charge."

Mei: "Okay, that's fine."

Mei took off the towel she was wearing and tossed it to Paul, leaving her completely naked.

Mei: "What about now? I'll dance for you naked, but we won't have sex."

Paul was silent for a moment while staring at Mei's nude body.

Paul (snapping out of his lusty silence): "No sex, I got it."

Despite Mei's lack of dancing skills, she managed to dance until Paul was relieved of his sexual desire.

[Scene 123]

[6 a.m.]

Mei lay on the bed in the guest room, ready to leave. She had only slept for an hour after dancing for Paul.

From the window of the room where she slept, she saw the reflection of headlights pulling into the driveway.

[Scene 124]

Paul must have gone out while Mei was asleep, because the car she saw in the driveway was the same one that had picked her up earlier at Allen Station. She went downstairs to investigate.

[Scene 125]

Paul was returning from a nearby 7-Eleven with three cartons of eggs and a gallon of milk.

Paul: "Morning."

Mei: "Good morning."

Paul: "I went to buy breakfast for all of us, especially for my two guests leaving today."

Mei: "You have another guest in the house?"

Paul: "Yes. You and your snake. Every snake in the basement swallows two cooked egg yolks for breakfast every morning. So, give me about thirty minutes to prepare breakfast, and then I'll drop you off at the station. How do you plan to transport the snake?"

Mei: "I'll carry it in my backpack."

Paul: "That backpack is too tight for transporting a snake . . . er . . . I'll give you one of my snake boxes."

Mei: "Thanks."

[Scene 126]

[Sixteen days had passed since Jason had fallen sick]

The doctors at Reno Hospital had discovered how the Tiamat sickness slowly killed the victim, yet they still couldn't figure out how to cure the disease.

The victim slowly lost blood, which, if not replaced, would result in death. Hence, they constantly had to give blood to Jason on a daily basis to keep him alive.

Mr. Jones had hired some of the best physicians in the nation to watch Jason around the clock, seven days a week.

Every member of the Jones family had donated blood; still, the rate at which Jason was losing blood meant that he required more blood donors.

Finding a blood donor was easier for Mr. Jones's medical researchers. Finally, on a daily basis, there was more blood available for Jason than the heart of every employee at Reno Hospital could pump in a week.

[Scene 127]

At the research center in Manhattan, the search for a perfect volunteer for the remedy continued. Finding a virgin to try Akar's cure had proven difficult, and unless there was an immediate intervention, Jason had less than a week to live. Bryan and the mayor advised Mr. Jones to call off the search and prepare his mind for Jason's death.

Mr. Jones was not going to give up until it was over, though. In a couple of days, he would be hosting two royal families from the Middle East and a bunch of prestigious clients from around the world. At that time, he would give an open speech that would raise his offer to a whole new level. The mayor would also bring the Tiamat Stone to the gathering and talk about it in public for the first time.

[Scene 128]

Back in Virginia, Mei mailed the letters she'd written to Jason and her parents before boarding the 2 p.m. bus back to New York. On the bus, her sunglasses covered her eyes. Her snake was concealed in a snake box.

There was a group of Chinese natives on board who spoke the language that Mei understood. She sat quietly, close to the window, looking at the countryside. Everything around her reminded her of home.

Mei was lost in a daydream when a Chinese guy, Hin, touched her arm. They conversed in Chinese.

Hin: "Are you from Beijing?"

Mei: "No."

Hin: "Why are you crying?"

Mei (with a faint smile while wiping her eyes): "I'm not crying. I'm just thinking about home."

Hin: "Why don't you call home and speak to your family?"

Mei: "I wish I could, but I don't have a cell phone."

Hin: "Here, use mine."

Mei took Hin's cell phone.

For the second time since she'd arrived in the United States, Mei spoke to her sister in China. Her father was terribly sick. The hospital bills were so high they'd sold almost everything in their house, and it still wasn't enough to cover them. KimCathy had called and informed the family that Mei was no longer staying with the company. Everyone at home was worried about her.

After she spoke to her sister, Mei was more determined to go back home. The moment she was done with Akar's cure, she would return to China; that is, if the cure didn't kill her.

Hin and the rest of his group were in the U.S on vacation. They would be returning to China in two days. Mei used that opportunity to send another note to her parents in Boluo. For the remainder of the trip, until the bus arrived in Brooklyn, the members of the Chinese group acquainted themselves with Mei.

[Scene 129]

Mei rode a bus to the part of Manhattan she was familiar with.

After the Virginia trip, she had thirty dollars and an inland taipan. The blue light in her eyes was still there, too.

You didn't have to be a magician to know that Mei was either stressed or stranded. Her slightly swollen eyes from the constant crying and her disheveled appearance showed evidence of that. On top of that, a heavy rain in Manhattan had drenched her that afternoon before she arrived at Bryan's office.

CATAPHRASE E

"Just like trouble, if look for peace you'll find it."

—Teni A.

[Scene 130]

[Gothan ballroom]

At the Gothan, a grand ballroom in Manhattan, hundreds of royal guests, business moguls, famous physicians, princes, and princesses from all corners of the world had gathered for the annual event that Mr. Jones hosted at the end of the year.

The New York City mayor, Bryan White, and the "wired" professor from the Albany Museum of Art were also there to talk about the effect of the Tiamat Stone.

Mrs. Jones had invited a lot of beautiful virgins to the occasion, along with Amy's friends who claimed to be virgins. The majority of guests invited by Mrs. Jones had come from overseas, mostly from wealthy families.

The annual event started as usual. First, every royal guest was introduced, followed by business moguls and then every other important guest. Mr. Jones would usually organize live entertainment for the partygoers, but this year would be different. Instead of entertainers, he'd invited various physicians. Most of them were already in New York looking after Jason, so he'd figured he should invite them.

The Tiamat Stone was placed in the center of the room in a show-box. An auction usually followed the event's speeches each year, which left many people thinking the Tiamat Stone was a precious item to be bid on later.

After the introduction speech, Mr. Jones stood up to speak.

Mr. Jones: "I want to thank all of you once again for joining my family to celebrate this annual event. It's my pleasure having you as guests.

"It's been a great and successful year so far for me and most of my business partners seated here today.

"I've thanked the Royal Emirates earlier, but I would love to thank them once again for allowing us to add another refinery in the Middle East. Thank you very much; it's a great pleasure working with you.

"Especially, I want to thank the mayor of New York City for his support and encouragement.

"My family and I know a time like this only comes once a year. That's why we always try to make it a memorable event for all of you. However, things don't always go as planned. In the midst of my success this year, I faced certain challenges. Some of these challenges were within my power to solve, and some of them are beyond my power.

"For those of you who are thinking the green stone in that show-box is for sale, I hate to disappoint you, but it is not. That stone is called Tiamat. I'm going to invite Professor Anthony, who knows more about the stone, and one of my private physicians, Bryan White, to tell you a brief history about the Tiamat Stone and why it is here today. Professor?"

Professor Anthony took the stage.

Professor Anthony: "Howdy. It's a great honor to be among all of you. I want to thank Mr. Jones and his beautiful wife for their gracious gesture toward the Albany Museum of Art. Mr. Jones, thanks for having me here.

"As the book written by an unknown pharaoh details it, the story of the Tiamat Stone began in Egypt, in a great city called Memphis.

"In 3000 B.C., after Osiris, an ancient god in Egypt, was betrayed and left to die in the Nile River by his own brother, it was Tiamat, the primordial goddess of sea water, who delivered him.

"The encounter between Osiris and Tiamat brought Tiamat to the earth's surface for the first time. Osiris convinced Tiamat to follow him farther on land, but Boreas, the god of the wind, wouldn't allow the beautiful goddess to enter the great city of Memphis unless she left her poisonous power behind. Instead of going back to the water, Tiamat decided to deposit her poison inside a stone before following Osiris into the city. She never returned.

"During a war between Tiamat and her husband's murderer, she was slain by Enki's son, the storm god Marduk.

"The stone where Tiamat deposited her poisonous power that day is what you are looking at here today.

"Many years after Tiamat's death, an American deep-sea diver, in the early forties, found the Tiamat Stone at the bottom of the ocean and brought it to New York City.

"Folks, I know some of you don't believe in mythology, just like me; however, everyone who has come into contact with the Tiamat Stone, including myself, can't deny the fact that there's something strange about it. I'm going to invite Dr. Bryan to tell you about the effect of touching the

Tiamat Stone and why it is here today."

Dr. Bryan took the stage.

Bryan: "Hello, everyone. It's a great honor to be among you. Like one famous writer said, 'Not everything that glitters is gold.' I know many of you, when you first saw the Tiamat Stone, thought to yourself, 'A big, precious, glittering stone like this must be very expensive.' That was the same thing I said when I first saw the stone.

"However, the Tiamat Stone is not precious. In fact, 'precious' and 'good' have nothing to do with it. Forget about the greenish, glittering appearance, which makes it seem attractive. Every story and legend told about the Tiamat Stone is true.

"In these stories, it's said that anyone who touches the Tiamat Stone will be infected with a deadly disease. We've checked this fact with the families of twenty people who have touched the stone to this date, and it's true. They were all infected with the same type of strange disease. But don't panic, because, in the same story, it was also written that a cure exists for the disease. Though we haven't yet tried the cure on a human, we've tried it on a rabbit, and it partially works.

"I used the word 'partially' because the nature of the cure is such that only a human can perform it.

"If you look at those four big screens to my left, you will see some words written on each screen in different languages: English, French, Arabic, and Spanish. That is the cure for the Tiamat disease.

"It was originally written in Arabic by a sorcerer named Akar Amos. Thanks to Professor Anthony for this; he is the one who worked on the translation from Arabic to English."

Prof. Anthony nodded happily where he sat.

Bryan: "As you read Akar's cure, I know the details might startle you a bit, especially regarding what it requires a virgin to go through.

"The words highlighted in yellow are what we tried on a rabbit. Many physicians who are in this room can testify to it. We injected two drops of venom from an inland taipan into the body of a rabbit infected with the Tiamat disease, and for the first time, we discovered that the venom of a snake such as the inland taipan is not always as dangerous as we thought. In this case, when the venom entered the blood vessel of the infected rabbit, it worked to neutralize the Tiamat poison.

"The rabbit, however, died due to the fact that, according to what you see on the screen, the complete cure can only be performed by a human.

"So, why is Tiamat stone here today? So much has happened since this stone surfaced again in Manhattan after many years in the ocean. A little less than three weeks ago, someone from Mr. Jones's family touched the Tiamat Stone.

"I believe some of you have heard about what happened to Jason, one of Mr. Jones's sons. He's the one who touched the stone. For those of you who are here for Mr. Jones's medical offer, this is what the offer is about. It's either now or never. Mr. Jones is willing to offer two hundred million dollars to any woman who will volunteer for Akar's cure."

Mr. Jones interrupted Bryan while walking to the podium.

Mr. Jones: "FIVE HUNDRED MILLION DOLLARS. I will give five hundred million dollars to any woman who volunteers. And that's not all. My wife Sharon and I will make sure, with every power within our might, that Jason will marry the woman who helps to save his life. *Five hundred million dollars*, anyone?"

There was a pin-drop silence in the ballroom. A lot of wealthy people in the room weren't worth three hundred million dollars. For a moment, everyone looked around to see if someone would respond to the offer.

When no one did, Mr. Jones raised his offer to a staggering one billion dollars. The reaction to the unexpected offer was speechlessness and astonishment.

If Professor Anthony had had a virgin daughter, he would have raised his hand on her behalf. His huge magnifying glasses had come off at the mention of a billion dollars.

Mr. Jones waited for about a minute, until it was apparent that no one was willing to volunteer. He decided to continue with the event.

Mr. Jones: "Okay, I understand. I want to thank all of you who came on behalf of Jason. Thanks for your time and concern."

As the guests were turning their faces side to side, still anticipating a response, the sound of someone struggling with the security guards was heard from the entrance to the ballroom. Someone was trying to force his or her way in.

[Scene 131]

As the nine-figure silence was wrapping up in the room, the double doors behind the ballroom were suddenly flung open.

Everyone looked back, in the direction of the door, and saw Mei walking forward, wearing sunglasses. She carried a box-shaped sack in her right hand. Her appearance was similar to a homeless person's.

All the guests in her path moved out of their seats. Mrs. Jones was the first to speak.

Mrs. Jones: "Security, get that filthy girl out of this room now."

As the unarmed security guard following Mei moved closer to grab her, she took off her sunglasses. The shining blue glow in her eyes sent the guards back and left everyone in amazement.

She removed the sack covering the transparent box, holding it in her right hand. An angry brown snake writhed around inside.

Professor Anthony, Dr. Bryan, and everyone who had read Akar's cure understood right away what Mei had been through and what she was ready to do.

With the transparent snake box still in her hand, Mei ran towards the Tiamat Stone, opened the show-box used to cover it, and picked up the green devil.

Immediately after touching the stone, she stuck her hand in the transparent box, and the inland taipan bit her twice before she fell to the ground. Dr. Bryan, Mr. Jones, and every physician in the room ran to her aid.

Bryan: "Someone call an ambulance."

Mr. Jones: "How many times was she bitten?"

Dr. Bryan looked at Mei's hand.

Bryan: "Twice."

Professor Anthony stood close by with a copy of Akar's cure, reading the seventh page in the book.

Professor Anthony: "After the snake bites the infected virgin, the glory of Mzui will leave his or her eyes."

Bryan checked both of Mei's eyes, and the blue light was no longer there.

Bryan: "Her heartbeat is increasing fast. I'm performing mouth-to-mouth resuscitation. Doctor, keep your hands on her feet. Let me know if her temperature is decreasing."

Physician (standing close to Mei): "I got it."

Bryan (in between giving mouth-to-mouth resuscitation)**:** "Can someone please secure that snake box? Professor?"

Professor Anthony (shivering): "I've a confession to make. I'm allergic to venomous snakes. In 1985, I was diagnosed with anaphylaxis. Despite my blood genotype allele, my doctors said I'm still vulnerable to wheezing from snake antigens, anaphylactic shock, and sudden heart or respiratory failure. The deleterious effect of seizure on my blood pressure is disastrous. In addition, I—"

Mr. Jones interrupted Professor Anthony by securing the snake box and handing it over to one of his bodyguards.

Mr. Jones: "The snake is secured. Bryan, what's going on?"

Bryan: "Her breathing is fine. It looks like she's asleep."

Physician: "We have to wake her up."

Professor Anthony: "Paramedics are here."

Two paramedics arrived on the scene.

Paramedic 1:"What happened to her?"

Bryan: "She got bitten by a snake."

Paramedic 2:"Did anyone see what kind of snake bit her?"

Professor Anthony: "It's right there in that box."

Professor Anthony pointed to the guard holding the snake box.

Paramedic 1: "Jesus. . . . What kind of snake is that?"

Professor Anthony: "Oh boy! You don't wanna know."

Paramedic 1: "All right, since we have it secured, the snake will have to come with us to the hospital. That's the fastest way we can find out what anti-venom she needs."

Bryan: "I need you guys to transport her to Reno State Hospital. My name is Bryan White. I'm a doctor. I have to come with her in the ambulance."

Paramedic 2: "We won't allow you to get in the ambulance with a patient. It's against our policy. You can follow the ambulance in your car."

Bryan: "That's fine; the snake will come with me in my car."

Professor Anthony (to Bryan): "Don't forget, the same snake that bit the virgin twice must also bite the victim twice."

Bryan: "Thanks, I won't forget."

[Scene 131]

Dr. Phillip, who was staying with Jason for the evening, was watching a baseball replay on a flat-screen TV in Jason's room when Bryan, Mr. and Mrs. Jones, and three more doctors burst through the door. Dr. Phillip plunged out of his seat.

Dr. Phillip: "What's going on?"

Bryan: "How is his blood pressure?"

Dr. Phillip: "It's 140 over 90. His blood pressure has been normal throughout the day. Is that a snake in your hand?"

Bryan (to Pence, another doctor at Reno Hospital): "Doctor, get the anti-venom ready. This has to be done in the emergency room in case things don't go as we expect."

Dr. Pence: "Not until Mr. Jones signs these documents here."

Bryan: "What's in the document?"

Dr. Pence: "That Mr. Jones understands the risk involved in this process. And he also understands that Akar's cure is not in any way scientific. Thus, no physician in this hospital shall be held responsible for whatever happens to Jason. And last, as one of Jason's parents, he must authorize the cure to be performed at this hospital at his own risk."

Mr. Jones (to Pence): "Where do you want me to sign?"

Dr. Pence: "Right here in the bottom, where it says, 'I have read and understand the content in this document.'"

Without hesitation, Mr. Jones signed the two-page document.

Mr. Jones: "Bryan, where is the snake handler you called earlier?"

Bryan: "He's five minutes away."

[Scene 132]

A security guard walked Scott, the snake handler, through the hallway to Jason's room. Scott thought he had been called there to remove a snake from the hospital.

[Scene 133]

Security Guard (to Bryan): "Doctor, your handler is here."

Bryan: "Let him in."

Scott entered the room.

Scott: "Hello, sorry I'm late. Where did you find the pet?"

Bryan: "It's not a pet. It's a snake."

Scott: "That's what I call them."

Bryan: "I need you to get to work right away. That's your pet right there in that box."

Scott: "You captured it already. Interesting. What kind of snake is this?"

Scott moved closer to the box.

Bryan: "It's an inland taipan."

Scott: "*No . . . way*. Unless this hospital is located in Australia, an inland taipan should not be found anywhere around here. Oh my God, it's a taipan. Where did you find it?"

Bryan: "Where we found it is not the problem. We brought it here for medical purposes. Scott, what we need you to do is not complicated. I want you to make that taipan bite the patient on this bed twice, that's all."

Scott: "I don't think you understand what you are asking me to do. One bite from a taipan is the same as fifteen bites from a rattlesnake. That one bite is also equal to ten bites from a king cobra. In summary, one bite from a taipan is enough to kill all of us in this room ten times over."

Mr. Jones: "We are not oblivious to everything going on around us. We know how dangerous a bite from a taipan could be. Yet what my doctor asked you to do is what we need you to do. That snake has to bite this boy twice, and it has to happen now."

Scott: "I don't know what to tell you, sir. I've never received such an assignment before. My job is to remove snakes, not make them bite people. I have a license for this job, you know. I could lose my license if anything bad happens to him."

Bryan: "Nothing bad will happen to him or your license. I'm a medical doctor. I took an oath to save human lives. If I thought what I'm asking you to do would hurt anyone in any way, I wouldn't allow it to happen. Scott, I just need you to trust me."

Mr. Jones: "Scott, how old are you?"

Scott: "I'm thirty-two."

Mr. Jones: "Do you have a wife, kids?"

Scott: "I'm married. I have a son. He will be three next week."

Mr. Jones wrote something down on a booklet he'd removed from his pocket.

Mr. Jones (to Scott): "How do you spell your last name?"

Scott: "Flores. F-L-O-R-E-S."

Mr. Jones handed a check over to Scott.

Mr. Jones: "Scott, that's a two-hundred-thousand-dollar check in your name. Use it for your son's birthday. Now, this patient here is my son. He won't be able to celebrate his next birthday unless this snake bites him twice. Scott, are you going to help me or not?"

Scott stared at the figures on the check in disbelief.

Scott: "Which part of his body do you want the snake to bite?"

Mr. Jones: "Anywhere, I don't care. Just make sure the snake bites him twice."

Bryan: "His leg. Let the snake bite him in the leg."

Scott carefully brought out the taipan with a snake rod and placed it close to Jason's foot. He then provoked the taipan until the angry snake bit Jason twice in the leg. Scott returned the snake back to the box when the job was done.

Scott: "Is that all?"

Bryan: "That's all."

Scott: "I hope he gets better. Thanks for the money, Mr. Jones."

Mr. Jones: "Thanks, Scott. Thanks for your help."

Scott: "You're welcome, sir. And good luck to your son."

A beep from an electrocardiogram monitoring Jason's heart distracted the conversation. The high-frequency reading on the screen indicated Jason's heart was beating fast. Jason shook abruptly on the bed where he was lying.

A doctor excused Mr. Jones and Scott from the room while the rest of them got to work on Jason. Every health-monitoring device attached to Jason produced high-frequency readings before going back to normal.

The situation lasted four minutes. Jason was asleep. His heavy sweating was a sign he was recovering. It was the third time Dr. Bryan had seen this happen. He had seen it happen to a rabbit, to Mei, and now to Jason.

Dr. Bryan confirmed Jason's recovery with Dr. Pence once again before going to the next floor to check on Mei.

[Scene 134]

Mei was awake. The doctors at Reno State Hospital had never seen anything like it before—for someone to be bitten twice by the world's deadliest snake and recover in under an hour without receiving anti-venom or treatment was nothing short of miraculous. It seemed, after all, that Akar's cure was real.

A nurse examined Mei's pupils by shining a light into her eyes. Her retina showed no signs of infection. Mei had no form of identification on her, so none of the nurses knew her name or where she lived.

Another nurse had just delivered a sandwich to Mei when Bryan and Mr. Jones walked into the room.

Bryan (to the nurse examining Mei): "How is her temperature?"

Nurse: "Great. Her body hasn't exhibited any negative reaction to the venom since she woke up."

Bryan: "Can we talk to her?"

Nurse: "Sure."

Bryan (to Mei): "Hi, my name is Dr. Bryan. What is your name?"

[Silence]

Mr. Jones's eyes bore into Mei. She looked up and met his gaze.

Mr. Jones: "Aren't you the lady I met at the dinner table a week or two before Jason fell sick? Mei, she is the maid who was with Jason at the abandoned house where Jason touched the stone."

Bryan: "Mei, how old are you?"

Mei: "Nineteen."

Bryan: "I want to assume you're a virgin. And with what you've done so far, I believe you've read Akar's cure and you know what's next in the cure. The victim must copulate with the virgin to consummate the cure. In the meantime, do you want to talk to anyone? We can call your parents to meet you here."

Mei: "Where is Jason?"

Bryan: "He's fine. He should be awake soon."

Mei: "Let me know when Jason is awake. I'm ready."

Mei gazed at the cell phone in Bryan's hand.

Mei: "Can I use your phone, please? I want to talk to my parents in China."

Bryan: "Sure, but the plan I have doesn't allow me to make international calls."

Mr. Jones: "Use mine."

Mei spoke in Chinese throughout the duration of the phone call. Neither Bryan nor Mr. Jones understood a word she was saying.

At one point during the call, the cell phone fell from Mei's hand while it was still close to her face. Tears rolled down her cheeks as the hand came down slowly.

Mr. Jones: "Are you okay? What happened?"

Bryan: "Why are you crying?"

Mei didn't say a word; she just kept crying. She ran to the bathroom, took off her clothes, and came back to the room wearing a white towel.

Mei (to Dr. Bryan and Mr. Jones): "I'm ready."

Bryan: "All right, let's do it."

[Scene 135]

Mei was taken to a surgery room that the doctors had prepared for the final part of Akar's cure to take place.

After an hour of sleeping, Jason woke up hale and hearty. But the greenish glow in his eyes was still there.

Bryan wasted no time taking Jason to the surgery room to meet Mei. There, he explained to him the nature of Akar's cure.

The room was left to Mei, Jason, and the doctors who would stand by in case anything went wrong.

[Scene 136]

The time approached midnight. Gary and Amy arrived at the hospital.

Everyone waited anxiously in the hallway outside the room.

Thirty minutes passed, and then an hour. A call came over the radio requesting Dr. Pence to report to the lobby. Someone from KimCathy wanted to see Mei.

Mr. Jones (to Dr. Pence): "Doctor, would you mind checking on them before you leave?"

Dr. Pence had just lifted his hand to knock on the door when the door handle turned. The sound of the opening door, though small, was heard by everyone in the hallway. Jason was the first to emerge from the room. Bryan checked Jason's eyes immediately, and the greenish glow was no longer there. At last, Jason was free from Tiamat's bondage. Mei came out shortly after Jason. Her white towel was stained with blood. She felt embarrassed by the way everyone stared at her. A second announcement came over the radio requesting that Dr. Pence report to his office.

[Scene 137]

[The following day, inside Mei's room at the hospital]

KimCathy had assumed Mr. Jones was now Mei's guardian. A representative from the company had brought Mei's property to the hospital the day before. They'd also delivered the news of her father's death in China. Mei was in her room crying. Mr. and Mrs. Jones brought their condolences and the reward they'd promised to give the volunteer.

Mrs. Jones: "Mei, I hope you can forgive me for the way I've treated you. I'm sorry for everything I have done wrong. I was devastated when I heard the news of your father's death. Please, accept my apology and my condolences."

Mr. Jones: "Here is the check I promised to give the woman who helped save Jason's life. One billion dollars."

Mr. Jones held the check out to Mei.

Mr. Jones: I've arranged for a lawyer to help you open an account and make sure you don't have any problem collecting the money. I'm grateful for all you've done for me and my family."

Mei: "I don't want the money."

Mr. Jones: "Don't worry, Mei, I promise you won't encounter any problem transferring the funds. You can have it. It's yours."

Mei: "I don't want it."

Mr. Jones: "What do you want?"

Mei: "I want to go home. I want to go back to China."

Mr. Jones: "That's not a problem. I can arrange for the money to be deposited in any account you want in China. I can also tell my pilot to take you home in one of my private jets. Do you have a bank account in China?"

Mei: "I don't want the money. I'd love to have my necklace back. When I save enough money, I'll go back home."

Mr. Jones: "You are refusing a billion-dollar check?"

Mei: "Yes, all I want is my necklace."

Mr. Jones: "I'm not sure what necklace you are asking for. Did you forget it in our house before you left there?"

Mrs. Jones: "I know what she wants. I left it in the white Rolls-Royce the day I collected it from her."

Mr. Jones: "The one outside?"

Mrs. Jones: "Yes."

Mrs. Jones told Amy to bring the diamond necklace upstairs. Some moments later, Amy returned and handed the necklace to Mrs. Jones. Mrs. Jones moved closer to Mei and placed the necklace around her neck.

Mrs. Jones: "I'm sorry for the misunderstanding."

Mrs. Jones's fingers curled around the necklace string. She admired the precious stone for a moment.

Mrs. Jones: "It's a diamond necklace. It's precious."

Mei: "A diamond isn't precious until a woman wears it."

[Silence]

Dr. Bryan: "When do you plan to go back to China?"

Mei: "When I save enough money."

Bryan: "Do you have a place to go from here?"

Mei (with tears)**:** "I don't know."

Bryan: "Mei, you do understand that, according to the cure, you can't have sex with any other man except Jason, or else the person will die."

[Silence]

Mr. Jones: "I've spoken to Jason about the other promise I made to the women who volunteered for the cure. I will get back to you as soon as I get a response from him."

[Silence]

Mrs. Jones: "Mei, I hope you understand it's a hard task for a parent to force their child to love a stranger. Jason needs more time to think about it."

[Scene 137]

Jason (entering the room): "I already did."

Jason had something in his pocket as he approached Mei.

Jason: "I'll go wherever Mei goes."

Amy (with a smile): "And if she goes back to China?"
Jason: "I'll go to China. I'll go wherever she goes."

Jason knelt in front of Mei while holding her hand.

Jason: "They say the most important thing in life is happiness. But you make me understand that happiness without love is like a prisoner who wins the lottery.

"I've always thought silver and gold were precious until I met you. You make me see how worthless stones are if a woman is not wearing them.

"I gave you a diamond necklace, and in return, you gave me life. Now it's clear to me that the beauty of life is not what someone achieves in life or what a person can achieve with life, but life itself.

"Life is precious, yet you risk yours to save mine. For this reason, I've decided to spend the rest of my life with you. No matter the circumstances that life could bring, I promise I'll be by your side. I'll cherish you, I'll adore you, and I'll love you every day of your life until death do us part."

Jason reached into his pocket and brought out a thirty-eight-karat diamond ring.

Jason: Mei, will you marry me?"

A song by K-Ci and JoJo, "All My Life," came on the overhead radio.

Everyone in the room was moved to tears. Mei, as usual, nodded her reply to Jason's proposal.

THE END